"Who is it I remi

A muscle jerked in the firm jawline. "What makes you think you remind me of anyone?"

"The way you've acted since we first met."

There was a hint of cruelty in the curl of his lip. "You mean my failure to make the approach you were anticipating?"

"I was anticipating nothing," Kirsten denied. "You leave me cold!"

"Is that so?" he said softly.

KAY THORPE was born in Sheffield in 1935. She tried out a variety of jobs after leaving school. Writing began as a hobby, becoming a way of life only after she had her first completed novel accepted for publication in 1968. Since then she's written over fifty novels, and lives now with her husband, son, German shepherd dog and lucky black cat on the outskirts of Chesterfield in Derbyshire. Her interests include reading, hiking and travel.

A Reckless Attraction

KAY THORPE

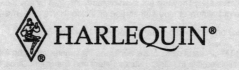

HARLEQUIN®

TORONTO • NEW YORK • LONDON
AMSTERDAM • PARIS • SYDNEY • HAMBURG
STOCKHOLM • ATHENS • TOKYO • MILAN • MADRID
PRAGUE • WARSAW • BUDAPEST • AUCKLAND

ISBN 0-373-80522-5

A RECKLESS ATTRACTION

First North American Publication 2000.

Copyright © 1993 by Kay Thorpe.

This edition published by arrangement with Harlequin Books S.A.

® and TM are trademarks of the publisher. Trademarks indicated with
® are registered in the United States Patent and Trademark Office, the
Canadian Trade Marks Office and in other countries.

Visit us at www.eHarlequin.com

Printed in U.S.A.

CHAPTER ONE

BOARDING would begin at eight o'clock, the ferry check-in clerk had said. Finding a seat in the crowded departure lounge had been difficult enough to start with; leaving it in order to get a cup of coffee from the bar would obviously result in losing it. A case of stay, stand or go thirsty, Kirsten reflected. It wasn't much of a choice.

People were still arriving for the eight-thirty sailing. Both English and Norwegian, with more than a few Americans, to judge from the snatches of conversation she kept picking up. Backpackers too, looking for the most part in dire need of a wash and brush-up. The man who had just found standing space in front of her sported several weeks' growth of beard along with the mandatory jeans and T-shirt. A regular Viking, with his thick sweep of sun-streaked blond hair and hunky build. He had need of those broad shoulders to carry a pack that size.

Almost as if catching her thought, he released the waist strap, narrowly missing her feet as he let the pack settle to the ground.

'*Beklager*!' he said, glancing round at her involuntary exclamation. The vivid blue eyes narrowed as they rested on her upturned face. Apparently recognising her origins, he added in English, 'I didn't see you there.'

It would have been difficult through the back of his head, she thought caustically. Not unaccustomed to such masculine evaluation, and usually capable of remaining unresponsive to it, there was something in this man's studied appraisal that made her bristle.

She held his gaze for a challenging moment before returning her attention to the phrase book she had been flicking through. Norwegian wasn't the easiest of languages to learn; the spelling seemed to have little bearing on the pronunciation. Not that she was going to have any difficulty in a country where most people spoke English as a second language anyway.

Nine days wasn't long in which to re-establish a relationship allowed to lapse for sixty odd years, she had to admit, but it could be a start. No matter how diluted her Norwegian blood, it was still a part of her. A very important part. Her name alone was a constant reminder of that heritage. She had told neither of her parents what she was up to. So far as they knew, she was taking a holiday in France with friends. If she failed in her quest there was no harm done.

The Norwegian backpacker had turned away again, thank heaven; those eyes of his could penetrate steel! She stole another glance at him, allowing her gaze to drift down the tapering back to lean hipline and taut male buttock. His legs were long and straight in the close-fitting denim, thighs firm and muscular. Six feet tall at least, and honed to the very peak of fitness. He appeared to be on his own.

A man who preferred his own company, Kirsten decided. Self-sufficient, for sure, if he had spent the last few weeks camping out, as the pup tent strapped to his pack suggested. Norwegians were great outdoors people, by all accounts, summer *and* winter. Odd that he would choose to spend time over here, though, when his own country had so much to offer in the way of spectacle. She looked forward to seeing the fjords herself, although much would depend on the time element, of course. She would remain in Bergen until she had achieved some kind of liaison with her kith and kin—no matter what it took!

The Bruland shipping company was the place to start. Her cousin would surely not refuse to even see her. The company itself was well-known in the shipping world, having grown from a small family-run affair in the twenties to the major concern it was today. Perhaps the greatest danger lay in them thinking she was only after sharing in their good fortune, but it would be up to her to dissuade them from that view. She wanted nothing from them but recognition.

They were beginning to board, she realised, as the jam of people at the far end of the terminal hall started to move. There was no point in joining the crush. Her cabin was reserved anyway. She had paid the supplement for a higher-class cabin than the standard fare allowed for. Even one night on board would be one too many down in the bowels of the ship.

According to the schedule, they were due in to Bergen late the following evening. At this time of year, daylight would only just have given way to twilight, which itself could last through to the small hours, dependent on the weather. The midsummer solstice, with all its attendant celebrations, was only a few days away. By then she hoped to have things sorted out.

The Norwegian man was making no move to join the queue either. He had taken a seat further along the facing row as it emptied, stretching his legs with an air of staying put until the last possible minute. His relaxed attitude suggested a fairly frequent use of the ferry crossing. It would probably be safe enough, Kirsten conjectured, if she delayed her own boarding until he made a move.

She changed her mind when he glanced her way. There was every possibility that he might think she was hanging

back on purpose. Attractive enough despite his somewhat
unkempt appearance to have some drawing power, she had
to grant, but hardly the type she would go for herself. Her
tastes ran to the rather more sophisticated—the man-about-
town image.

Like Nick Foster? came the wry thought. He had been
all of that. Perhaps it was time she changed her tastes, and
found someone she could trust.

Gathering her things together, she got to her feet, ignoring the steady regard from across the aisle. Packed as it
was to cover all vagaries of the Bergen weather, her suitcase was both bulky and heavy. She lifted it with an effort,
regretting the lack of wheels. It would have been better if
she had used two smaller cases rather than the one large,
she realised. Too late now anyway.

The crowd about the exit doors had dwindled to man-
ageable proportions. She followed the last of them outside
and down a covered passage to emerge on the open wharf.
Towering above, the ship seemed enormous—more like a
cruise liner than a ferry. The gangway rising to the entry
deck looked too steep for comfort. A young woman in front
who was wearing high heels had difficulty in negotiating it
at all, making Kirsten thankful that she had elected to wear
low-heeled pumps herself. Not that she would have chosen
anything else to go with trousers, in any case.

Reaching the foot of the gangway, she paused to put the
suitcase down and flex fingers already numbed from the
pressure of the handle. It was going to be a struggle, but
short of yelling up for some help she would have to cope.

'I'll take that,' said a voice behind her in accents familiar
to her ear even though she had only heard them the once.

'I can manage,' she said without turning. 'You have
enough of your own to carry.'

'On my back, not in my hands,' he said. 'You'll find it easier with at least the one hand free to grasp the side-rail.'

It would be downright boorish, to say nothing of idiotic, Kirsten decided, to refuse the offer merely because he had made her hackles rise for a moment or two back there. At least he was capable of acting the gentleman even if he didn't look the part.

'Thanks,' she said, trying not to sound grudging about it. 'It's very thoughtful of you.'

'Isn't it?' he returned drily.

With just the occasional strip of wood nailed across to create footholds, the gangway proved a challenge even without the suitcase. She was glad to reach the top and step into the roomy reception area, where several uniformed stewards were directing the oncoming passengers to their various decks.

Coming up in her wake, the Norwegian deposited her suitcase to one side out of the way, but kept his pack on his back. He was an inch or two over the six-foot mark, Kirsten saw, now that she was able to measure her own height against him.

'Which cabin grade are you?' he asked.

She took another look at her ticket. 'N3.'

'Then we're on the same deck.' The blue eyes registered her involuntary surprise with a certain irony. 'Three flights up. Shall we go?'

'I don't need. . .' she began, then stopped as he lifted a sardonic eyebrow. In the absence of any other proffered assistance, of course she needed. 'Thanks,' she said again, and this time tried a smile to go with it. 'I'm grateful.'

He made no response, but simply picked up the suitcase again, wielding it as if it weighed next to nothing. Show-off! she thought scathingly, knowing she was being unfair. He wasn't trying to impress her.

The stairwell was through a pair of opened glass doors set into the far bulkhead. Whoever he was, the man certainly knew his way around, she thought, as she followed him up the carpeted flights. He seemed to be the only one with a backpack in this part of the ship, although most people were casually dressed. If he could afford the supplement, then he was certainly no indigent. But then he wouldn't be, would he, coming from where he did? Norway had one of the highest living standards in the world.

Their deck was one below boat deck. A comforting thought, regardless of the unlikelihood of anything going amiss. Alleyways stretching to either hand gave access to the cabins. Kirsten was somewhat relieved to discover that their relevant numbers lay along opposite arms, although her helper insisted on carrying the case to her cabin first.

The keys were in the lock. She opened the door and held it while he went in and lifted the suitcase on to a berth.

'As I said, I'm really grateful,' she told him. 'It would have been quite a struggle on my own.'

'I'm sure you'd always find someone to help you,' he returned. 'All you need to do is smile the right way.' He gave her a somewhat cursory nod. 'Enjoy your trip.'

She bit back the retort that trembled on her lips. Allowing this Norwegian philistine to rile her was stupid. Whether it was the English in general or English women in particular that he didn't care for was immaterial. He meant nothing to her, so why should she care what his opinions might be?

The cabin was an outside two-berth with shower and WC. It seemed unfair to have the other berth going spare when there were passengers on board without accommodation at all, but sharing with a stranger held little appeal either. She had been assured by the travel agent that the cabin was hers alone for the duration of the trip, and could only hope that the promise held true.

Showering in the confined space was no easy task, especially as the whole bathroom floor became covered in water due to the lack of a proper shower tray. She had packed a complete change of clothing uppermost in her case. Clad in black and white checked trousers and lightweight white sweater, she viewed her reflection in the bulkhead mirror and wondered if she could do with losing a few pounds. According to the charts, she was just about right for her height at eight and a half stone, but the magazines always gave the impression that anything above a size eight was heading for disaster.

Falling straight and heavy from its central parting to curve under at the ends where it touched her shoulders, her hair needed little attention beyond that supplied by comb and brush. Deep chestnut in colour, it made her eyes look greener than they actually were. She sometimes contemplated having it cut short for convenience, but it was such a drastic step. This style probably suited her face better than any wash-and-go bob anyway.

They had been underway for about fifteen minutes; she could feel the throbbing of the engines beneath her feet, the increasing movement. The North Sea in June shouldn't be too rough. At least she hoped not. She had never been seasick before, but this crossing was rather different from cruising in the Mediterranean or ferrying to France, which was all she had done up to now.

At nine o'clock she left the cabin to make her way down to the restaurant deck. The ship was packed, with people sitting, standing and even in some cases lying everywhere. Most were still in casual dress, Kirsten noted, with more than a sprinkling in shorts. The whole atmosphere of the ship was casual, if it came to that, although not lacking in creature comforts, by any means.

The restaurant itself was full, with several people already waiting for tables. Bypassing the glass windows of the ship's duty-free shop, now closed, she found the cafeteria awash with bodies too. It was self-service in here, which at least cut out the waiting time–always providing she could find a table. She wasn't really hungry enough to do justice to a full *koldtbord* in any case, and the price would be the same no matter how much or how little one ate. While not particularly limited, her budget had to cater for a much higher cost of living over the coming week and a half.

The queue proved orderly enough, the service fast and efficient. The hot food on offer was typical cafeteria fare and held little appeal. Kirsten settled for a couple of the open sandwiches called *smørbrød*, piled high with smoked salmon and egg. They would see her through until breakfast.

Precariously balancing her plate and a cup of coffee on a tray, she moved aft to look for a spare seat. There were plenty of tables but no shortage of occupants either–and all of them, it seemed, talking at the tops of their voices. The aisles themselves were thronged with people coming and going.

'Sit here, love,' said a broad Yorkshire voice behind her. 'We're just going.'

Kirsten put her tray down on the table with a sigh of relief, smiling her thanks at the middle-aged couple as they rose. She was aware of someone else sitting on the other side of the table, but it wasn't until she slid into one of the empty chairs and looked across that she realised who it was.

'Hello again!' she said with an assumed brightness. 'I hope you don't mind. There doesn't seem to be anywhere else at the moment.'

Her Norwegian helper was seated sideways in his chair, back leaning comfortably against the bulkhead, legs stretched out in the space where a fourth chair should have stood. He had on a clean T-shirt, Kirsten noted, but he still had the beard. His regard was impassive.

'So I see,' he said. 'You might have found the restaurant more suitable.'

'There was a queue. In any case, I didn't feel like a full meal.' She left it at that, annoyed with herself for finding it necessary to explain her reasons for being here, added lightly, 'This obviously isn't *your* first crossing?'

'No,' he agreed.

'Why travel to England,' she asked curiously, 'when your own country is so scenic? I'd have thought it would all seem very tame in comparison.'

'Apparently you never visited the high fells of your Yorkshire Dales or Lake District,' came the unhurried return. 'The landscape there is far from tame.'

'No, I didn't,' she admitted. 'I'm from the south.'

'Then you have Dartmoor and Exmoor–different in character, perhaps, but no less wild.' The pause was brief. 'You prefer indoor activities, perhaps?'

It was difficult to tell from his tone whether any innuendo was intended or not. Kirsten gave him the benefit of the doubt.

'Not necessarily. I just don't see the pleasure in living rough the way you've been doing–especially alone.'

He lifted an eyebrow. 'What makes you so sure I was alone?'

'Just a feeling. You strike me as someone who'd prefer his own company.'

'You study psychology?'

The mockery was faint, but enough to rile her again. It was an effort to keep her tone easy. 'As I said, it's just a feeling. Feminine instinct, if you like.' She cut into the first sandwich, aware of the blue eyes on her face. 'This looks so good! How does food in England compare with Norwegian?'

'There are many similarities. The main difference lies in preparation—and quantity. Meals tend to be much larger in Norway. We're an active race, and burn up a lot of energy—one way or another.'

She made the mistake of looking up, registering the derisive glint with a sudden tensing of her stomach muscles. Damn the man! she thought crossly. He had said nothing she could take righteous exception to, but the intimation was there all right. Well, two could play *that* game!

'I'm sure of it,' she said with a deliberately provocative little lift of her own eyebrow. 'You look fit for. . .anything!'

The glint became a spark, infinitely more disturbing. 'Looks can sometimes be deceptive.'

'In England,' she countered, 'we'd say "Never judge a book by its cover". Do you do much reading in your country?'

'Statistically, more than most other countries,' came the smooth return. 'Including England. How else would we entertain ourselves during the long dark winter evenings?'

You're way out of your depth with this one, said a small warning voice at the back of Kirsten's mind as she sought some adequate response. He could not only give as good as he got, but top her every time. She contented herself with a smile and a shrug, and concentrated her attention on the *smørbrød*.

What she couldn't shut out, however, was her awareness of his sheer masculinity; he exuded it from every pore. The muscular forearm he was resting on the table was deeply tanned beneath the light covering of pale gold hair, his hand well-shaped, with long clever fingers. Not a labourer's hand, for sure, although he seemed essentially the outdoor type. She wondered what he did do for a living.

'Your English is very fluent,' she remarked after a moment, needing to find something to say just to break the silence. 'Have you lived in England at all?'

He shook his head. 'You'll find many Norwegians who speak English fluently. It's a compulsory subject in school from the fifth grade onwards, and mixing with tourists, plus travel in your country, makes it easy to pick up the more informal way of speaking the language. The only places where you may have difficulty in making yourself understood would be in the more rural areas where the local dialects are still in use. Even then, you'll always find someone who can speak English.'

'Always assuming, of course, that I don't speak any Norwegian myself.'

'Do you?'

The scepticism was not without justification, Kirsten was bound to admit. All the same, it rankled. 'Enough to get by,' she claimed recklessly. 'In any case, I don't plan on making any field trips.'

'You'll be staying in Bergen the whole time you're in Norway?'

'Apart from going up to Flåm and Hardanger, perhaps. Since they're regular tourist haunts, I imagine all nationalities will be catered for there.' She added lightly, 'I'm not going to have time to travel all that far.'

'By road, perhaps not, but most places can be reached by air in a comparatively short time.'

'At a price.'

His head inclined. 'True. Norway is no place to visit on a tight budget.'

She hadn't meant to imply a shortage of funds, and resented his intimation that she shouldn't be here at all if she couldn't afford it. The ship's motion was becoming more pronounced, awakening a faint queasiness as she surveyed the second *smørbrød*. Eyes bigger than her stomach, she chided herself. One would have been enough.

'Is it likely to get any rougher than this?' she asked as the deck canted once more.

'The forecast was fair,' he said. 'There should be no problem. Do you suffer from seasickness?'

'Not up to now,' she acknowledged. 'But I suppose there's always a first time. I never crossed the North Sea before.'

'You can get dramamine from the medical room if you need it. It might be a good idea to take some in any case—prevention being better than cure.'

'I have some travel tablets with me,' Kirsten admitted. 'I meant to take some before I boarded, just in case, but I forgot.' She pushed her plate aside and stood up, avoiding direct contact with the vivid gaze. 'Prevention being better than cure, I'll go and do it now. Thanks for the. . .company.'

The rush for food was over, it seemed, with everyone now seated. Making her way along the aisle to the doorway, Kirsten tried to go with the movement of the ship, but was unable to stop herself from catching the top of her thigh on a table-edge in passing.

Aware that her erstwhile companion might be watching, she refrained from rubbing the injured spot, muttering imprecations to herself instead. There was no doubt at all that the motion was becoming more pronounced by the minute. No problem for him, perhaps, but definitely going to be one for her if she didn't do something about it quick.

She was feeling even worse by the time she reached her cabin. Uncovered, the large square port afforded a view of the rolling, white-capped sea. She drew the single curtain hurriedly across, then went to get a glass of water in order to take the two small white tablets she had left ready in her vanity case for just this event, hoping it wasn't too late.

It was all in the mind, she told herself, knowing it wasn't true. The best thing she could do was go to bed and hopefully to sleep. By morning, her balance should have adjusted itself.

Only morning was a long way off, and even the simple act of cleaning her teeth increased her queasiness. The very thought of the further movement involved in undressing was too much. She lay down on the berth as she was and tried to relax. So far, the tablets were having no effect, but they would, given the opportunity. What she mustn't do was give way to the nausea coming in waves that threatened to swamp her.

At which point she fell asleep, she had no idea. One moment it seemed she was lying there gritting her teeth, the next opening her eyes to find herself apparently free of all symptoms.

She sat up with caution, waiting for the malaise to strike again, but it didn't. Either the dramamine had worked, or her inner ear balance had adjusted itself to the motion on its own. The latter was certainly no less, although she didn't think it was any worse either. Finding one's sea legs even made it enjoyable.

According to her watch, it was just gone two o'clock in the morning, which meant she must have slept for nearly two hours. She felt wide awake now. Too much so to contemplate going to bed properly. Reading held little appeal either.

The port revealed a sky black as velvet and sparkling with stars, a sea rolling slow and deep, with only the occasional white-capped wave to break the pattern. Kirsten wanted suddenly to be out there, tasting the sea air, feeling the wind on her face, relishing her new-found freedom. There would be few other people around at this hour; she would probably have the whole upper deck to herself. It was hardly rough enough for there to be any danger of falling overboard.

She tied back her hair into the nape of her neck with a scarf to keep it out of her eyes, and donned the black and white jacket that went with her trousers. It was likely to be cool out there at night, regardless of the time of year.

The narrow alleyway outside the cabin was empty and silent, apart from the creaking sounds normal to any ocean-going vessel. From what she could recall of the plan of the ship located in the reception area, there was one other covered deck above this, giving access to boat stations, then the open top deck right above that. With the stairwell just around the corner, it should take no more than a minute or two to reach her objective.

She met no one on the stairs, although she could hear the sound of music coming from somewhere. There was a nightclub on board, she recalled from the ferry line's brochure, and a casino too. It was possible that the latter stayed open all night, she supposed; or at least while there were people still wanting to play. Gambling was addictive. Once started, some people just couldn't stop. Nick had been more than halfway there himself.

She was supposed to be forgetting about Nick, she reminded herself ruefully. Only it was easier said than done. At twenty-three, she was hardly in any imminent danger of being left on the shelf, but, with most of her friends already into steady relationships, she was beginning to feel the odd one out.

If she were truly honest with herself, she had known from the first that Nick wasn't all he made himself out to be, but she had closed her eyes and ears to the doubts, and persuaded herself that love could conquer all. If and when she did find someone else, it wouldn't be with any such romantic notion uppermost in mind. Personality was more important than looks, integrity of far greater value than an easy charm.

The glass panelled door leading out on to the open deck was heavily sprung to close automatically after use. It was certainly much cooler out here, but stimulating too, the air clean and fresh. Kirsten filled her lungs with it. So far as she could see, she was still alone in her desire for a night walk, although that wasn't to say she would find the upper deck empty. If some of the backpackers were without accommodation, as seemed likely from those she had seen lying around earlier, they might be using sleeping-bags up there out of the way. If so, she would leave them to it. Those who wanted to sleep were entitled to consideration.

An open gangway gave access to the upper deck. With little to block it, the wind felt much stronger up here, but not unbearably so. She moved aft to find a slightly more sheltered spot, leaning on the rail to view the swaying horizons with a swelling sense of well-being because she could do so with impunity now. A life at sea had a lot to recommend it. If she were a fully qualified dentist instead of just an oral hygienist, it might even be possible to get a job on board a cruise liner. It wasn't too late to start training—especially considering the two years she had already put in on dental hygiene.

On the other hand, she would be approaching thirty by the time she attained even the most basic qualification, which didn't appeal at all. Better in the long run to settle for what she had. The remuneration was good, and job itself interesting, and the practice employing her one of the best she knew of—to say nothing of the people she worked with.

Engrossed in her thoughts, she was startled enough to

almost jump out of her skin when a voice spoke behind her.

'If you feel ill, you should turn downwind.'

It would have to be, wouldn't it? she thought wryly. Was there no getting away from the man? She turned round slowly to seek out the figure reclining on a lounger set up behind the funnel superstructure a few feet away. Wearing a windcheater over his T-shirt now, the Norwegian returned her regard expressionlessly. His face looked chiselled from stone in the dim deck-lighting.

'I'm not feeling sick,' she denied. 'I was just enjoying the solitude. Couldn't you sleep either?'

'I didn't yet try.' He got to his feet, coming forward to join her at the rail. 'I needed some air after spending the last two hours in the casino.'

'Winning, or losing?' she queried lightly.

'I always play to win,' he said.

'Then I suppose it will be Buck's Fizz for breakfast!' she quipped.

He was gazing out to sea, mouth slanted. 'Is that the way *you* celebrate?'

The tone was a goad in itself. 'As a matter of fact,' she said coolly, 'I detest champagne—with or without the orange juice. Not that my lifestyle offers much opportunity, anyway.'

'Just an ordinary working girl?'

Not for anything, Kirsten decided, would she give him the satisfaction of letting him see her nettled by the derisive comment. She conjured a laugh. 'That's me!'

He gave her a sideways glance that lingered for just too long a moment in the region of her mouth, giving rise to the sudden and pulse-jerking suspicion that his whole attitude might well be nothing but a cover. Standing there, hair and beard glinting gold in the deck-lighting, shirt front stretched taut across muscular chest, he looked every inch the Viking. He stimulated her senses. Enough so to induce a sudden recklessness. She had never deliberately flirted in her life, but she found herself doing it now, putting out a hand to run the tips of her fingers lightly over the crisp hair lining his jaw.

'It's said that a kiss without a beard is like beef without mustard,' she murmured.

His upper lip curled. 'And you like *fransk sennep, ja*?'

The lapse into Norwegian was disconcerting, but not nearly as much as the steel-like grasp on her upper arms as he pulled her to him. His lips were hard, pressuring hers apart, his tongue a searing intrusion. Struggling to free herself, she felt both hands slide around her back to bring her into closer proximity, moulding her to him in a way that brought the blood pounding into her ears.

She stared at him in stunned silence when he put her abruptly away from him again, unable to think of a single thing to way.

'If you don't like the heat, stay out of the kitchen,' he advised. 'Isn't that also one of your sayings?'

Kirsten put out an unsteady hand to grip the rail as he left her standing there. She felt totally humiliated. How could she have acted that way at all, much less with a total stranger? It just wasn't like her.

She supposed she should feel fortunate that he'd seen fit to leave it at a kiss–although the invective he had managed to put into that alone had left an impression she was unlikely to forget in a hurry. She could still feel the unrelenting pressure of his mouth, the scorching probe of his tongue, the unyielding hardness of his body. Worst of all was the contempt she had seen in the blue eyes–particularly as it was so well deserved. She had acted like a common little tart!

It was several minutes before she finally forced herself
to move. The wind had sharpened, driving a chill into her
bones. Bad as she felt, it would be ridiculous to allow
this. . .incident to prey on her mind, she told herself firmly.
It in no way affected the purpose of her trip.

As to the Norwegian, he could go take a running jump.
Preferably over the side!

CHAPTER TWO

STANDING on the same deck some twenty hours later as the ship cruised the calm and sheltered waters of the Byfjorden, Kirsten devoured the passing scenery: rocky sea cliffs, tiny inlets and secret coves; clapboard houses painted all the colours of the rainbow outlined against a sky turning opaque as the day slowly faded.

This would have been her grandmother's last sight of her homeland, her last contact with people of her own kind. Disowned by her family for the sin of loving a man who was not of that kind. Just seventeen years old when she left, and only sixty-three when she died. It was to be hoped that the years between had been happy enough to make up for all she had lost.

There had been at least one attempt that Kirsten knew of by her father to make contact with the Norwegian branch of the family on his mother's death, but there had been no response. Although he often talked of it, he had never been able to bring himself to make any further effort, and his two married sisters showed no interest whatsoever. Which left it up to her, as the last of the Harley line, to try and heal the rift. She intended to give it her very best shot.

The wooded slopes of the seven hills on which Bergen was built came into view as the ship rounded a jutting point of pine-cloaked rock. Lights were beginning to gleam, marking out the houses, streets and highways along the shores and into the hills. A small fleet of fishing boats slid past, lamps twinkling at stern and bow, engines muted by the deeper throb of the larger vessel. The air felt cool on her skin, but not cold, smelling of sea and land together.

They docked on the periphery of the inner harbour. Kirsten lingered on deck for a final look at the picturesque quayside known as the Bryggen, with its gabled Hanseatic merchants' houses. Bergen was steeped in history. She looked forward to exploring it during the next few days. Even if she failed in her quest, it had been worth the journey just to be here. She had an odd sense of belonging.

Among the last of the passengers to disembark, she found herself at the tail end of the queue for taxis when she got outside the terminal building. The daylight was fading into twilight, soft and comforting. She didn't mind waiting. Her room was reserved, and the hotel would surely be aware of the ferry's arrival time. There would be a night porter on duty, anyway.

It was gone eleven when she finally reached the front of the line. The taxi driver spoke English, but was obviously thinking more of home and bed than conversation as he yawned his way along the waterfront. Looking back down the length of the Vågen, Kirsten could see the bulk of the ship she had left hugging the jutting quayside, her deck lights reduced now from their former Christmas-tree brightness to the same dim glow of the previous night. There would be several more such journeys back and forth before she was due to board again.

She had seen nothing of the Norwegian since he had left her on deck. Not that she had wanted to. If he came from Bergen itself, she supposed there was a chance that she might run into him again while she was here, but so what? She had more worthwhile things to think about than the remote possibility of finding herself in his company once more.

The Rosenkrantz hotel took its name from the street on which it was situated at the back of the Bryggen. The reception clerk still on duty welcomed her in English, and completed formalities in double-quick time.

Surveying the spacious and modern bedroom-cum-sitting-room with its television and mini-bar, Kirsten congratulated herself on having made a good choice of place to stay. Not exactly cheap, by her standards, perhaps, but spotlessly clean and nicely decorated. She had made the reservation for the full nine nights, but at this time of year they would have no difficulty in filling the room if she decided to move on, she was sure. That decision would come later, after she had tested the Bruland waters.

Just what she was going to say if and when she did get to meet her cousin she had no fixed idea as yet. All she could do was announce who she was and play it by ear from there. The whole affair had been two generations ago. Whatever the feeling engendered at the time, surely it was time now to let bygones be bygones?

Tired, she lost little time in unpacking her suitcase and preparing for bed. The *en-suite* bathroom had every convenience to hand. Clad in the satiny pyjamas she preferred to nightdresses, which always seemed to finish up around her neck, she slid between cool cotton sheets with a sigh of relief. A good night's sleep would put her in the right frame of mind to tackle whatever the day might throw at her. She doubted if it was going to be plain sailing.

Tired or not, sleep was some time in coming. Lying there, she found her thoughts turning inevitably to the previous night, reliving every moment of the encounter. It hurt even more to acknowledge that she had deliberately provoked the man. A part of her had wanted to know what it would be like to be kissed by that cynical mouth of his.

What she hadn't anticipated was the contempt he'd displayed. There had surely been no cause to go that far?

On the other hand, alone as they had been, he could have gone a whole lot further, she supposed, which seemed to indicate a total lack of interest. That thought rankled too, much as she hated to admit it. Not just demeaned but discarded out of hand. Coming on top of Nick's defection, it was certainly no boost to her ego.

Wide awake at seven despite her lack of sleep the night before, she took herself down to the waterfront, where the market traders were busy setting up for the day. Famous the world over, the fish market had every conceivable variety on offer. Some boats were unloading the night's catch right now, transferring it directly to the stalls. You couldn't, Kirsten thought, get much fresher than that!

Further along, where the local ferries were boarding daytrippers to the fjords and islands, van load after van load of flowers formed a multi-hued mosaic along the quayside, filling the air with fragrance. Once the ferries had departed, the view across the water to the old quarter was restricted only by the sky-scraping masts of the huge white yacht tied up at the Bryggen. The gabled warehouses seemed to lean towards each other across the narrow streets.

The sun lifted slowly into sight above the eastern heights, turning the flat oily calm of the harbour waters to sparkling gold, the hills themselves to verdant green. Pastel-coloured houses sprinkled the lower slopes, with one larger building perched in solitary splendour halfway up the nearest mountainside.

The Fløyen funicula terminal, Kirsten guessed, following the line down through the trees until it disappeared behind the houses. The view from up there was reputed to be one of the finest in the world, but it would have to wait. She had priorities more pressing than sightseeing.

As on board ship, breakfast at the hotel came in the shape of a self-service buffet with a vast variety of choice. Apart from the cereals and fruit juices, there were breads of all kinds, cheeses and jams, cold cuts of meat or fresh herring, and eggs both hard-and soft-boiled. Kirsten contented herself with fruit juice, bread and cheese, finishing off with a cup of the excellent coffee.

The hotel was busy. As would be the whole of Bergen at this time of year, the travel agent had warned her. Not just a port but a cultural centre too, with museums and art galleries by the score, to say nothing of the concert halls and theatres. It was a pity she had missed the International Festival, but then music was hardly the reason she was here.

And the sooner she did something about the reason she *was* here the better, she thought firmly, stifling any trepidation before it could take hold. The company offices lay in the modern section of the city across the Puddefjord; that much she knew from a perusal of the telephone directory and reference to the street map she had purchased at Reception. With no private address at hand, it was the only place to start.

Wearing a lightweight cream suit in a linen mixture resistant to creasing, she climbed into the taxi ordered for her by Reception feeling anything but confident. She was going to be barging in on someone who probably didn't even know of her existence. What kind of shock would it be for him to have her turn up on his doorstep, so to speak?

It would obviously be necessary to make some partial explanation to lower members of staff in order to stand any chance of reaching Leif Bruland at all; the company chairman was hardly going to be available to just anyone who asked to see him. But she *would* see him, no matter what! Having come this far, she had no intention of turning back without some kind of result. She owed it to her namesake, if to no one else.

The industrial section looked much like any other she had ever seen, if rather cleaner than most. Situated close by the fjord, the Bruland headquarters were housed in an imposing modern block that said all that needed to be said about company standing. Kirsten would have preferred some place a little less intimidating, but she hardly had a choice. The next half-hour or so was going to be the most difficult. After that remained to be seen.

There was a security guard on duty alongside the male receptionist. With no other obvious visitors in sight, the two of them watched her cross the half-acre of thick carpet to the long curved desk.

'My name is Harley,' she said clearly. 'Kirsten Harley. I'd like to see the chairman, please.'

The two men glanced at each other, then back to her with almost identical expressions. The receptionist was the first to speak.

'You have an appointment, Miss Harley?'

She shook her head, knowing what was coming even before the man began to form the words. 'I think if you tell him I'm his cousin from England, he'll want to see me,' she added quickly, only realising how odd that sounded after she had said it.

From the way he was looking at her, it was obvious that he thought so too. She summoned a smile. 'A surprise visit!'

The doubt still remained. 'If you will take a seat,' he said formally, 'I will enquire.'

There was little else she could do for the moment but wait for the result of that enquiry. Kirsten conceded, obeying the injunction. She certainly wasn't going to get past this point without agreement from above. She kept her expression carefully controlled as the man lifted a telephone. He spoke in Norwegian, of course, and fast, which made translation impossible, although she could recognise her own name. Neither he nor the guard took his eyes off her.

It seemed an age before he finally replaced the receiver. Kirsten had the feeling that he had spoken to more than one person. He would hardly have got straight through to Leif Bruland, in any case. More likely a secretary or PA.

'The chairman is engaged at present,' he announced, 'but the managing director will see you. Take the first lift over there to the seventh floor.'

'The managing director?' she queried. 'Is he a Bruland too?'

'Of course.' The man sounded even more nonplussed. 'He is the chairman's son.'

Kirsten could appreciate his puzzlement. If she really was Leif Bruland's cousin, then his son obviously had to be related too. It must seem strange that she hadn't even been aware of his designation. He would think it stranger still if she told him she hadn't even been aware of the son's existence.

She left him to work it out for himself, heading for the bank of lifts he had indicated. Father or son, it made little difference. He had consented to see her, which had to be something of an encouragement. The rest was up to her. She still had little idea of what she was going to say. There wasn't much point in preparing a speech when she hadn't even been sure she would be received at all. Thinking positive was one thing, doing quite another. If she'd been turned away this morning it would have taken a great deal of courage to try another approach.

The lift carried her upwards at high speed, leaving her

stomach at ground level. She felt decidedly queasy when she got out, although that was as likely to be caused by nerves as vertigo. She found herself on a large, open-plan office floor and faced by yet another reception desk, manned this time by a middle-aged woman who regarded her with frank curiosity.

'Mr Bruland is expecting you,' she said in the excellent English Kirsten was coming to take for granted. 'The door there on the left.'

Reaching it, Kirsten drew in a deep and steadying breath before lifting a hand to knock lightly on the rich dark teak. The answering voice was muffled by the thickness of the wood, but she took it as an invitation to enter.

Large, light and luxurious, the office beyond had a superb view over the fjord. The man seated at the big desk in front of the window was half swivelled away from her in his chair, telephone to ear. He waved his free hand in her direction without turning his head.

'Have a seat,' he said. 'I won't be a moment.'

Kirsten listened in frozen silence as he finished his conversation, watched him replace the receiver in its rest and steeled herself for the impact as he spun the chair back to face her directly. The shock wasn't hers alone, by any means. For a stunned moment or two he just sat there gazing at her, face registering a variety of expressions—none of them encouraging. When he did speak it was in low flat tones that were anything but friendly.

'You had better close the door.'

She did so, fingers nerveless. Minus the beard now, the lines of his face were clean and incisive, his jawline taut, mouth firmly cut. He was wearing a pale grey suit of impeccable taste, and looked every inch the executive. The blue eyes were like chips of ice.

'Am I to understand that *you* are Kirsten Harley?' he demanded.

Fate had a way of playing the most lousy tricks, she thought wryly. Who could have imagined this situation? It had happened, though, and she had to deal with it. She made a supreme effort to regain her equilibrium.

'The same,' she said. 'A small world, isn't it?'

'So it appears.' He came to his feet, moving round the desk with a lithe tread to indicate the small group of easy-chairs placed around a central table to one side of the spacious room. 'Sit down.'

It was more of a command than an invitation, but she was in no position to carp about inflexions. Shock was giving way to anger as she compared his appearance now with the way he had looked on board ship. It was as if he had deliberately set out to make a fool of her.

A ridiculous notion, of course. He could have had no more idea of her identity than she had had of his. They hadn't even exchanged names.

The chair she took was comfortable, but she was hardly in any mood for relaxation. He made no move to take a chair himself, but leaned his weight against the desk-edge to regard her with the same narrowed appraisal she had first undergone at the ferry terminal in Newcastle. The very fact that he stayed on his feet while she sat put her at a disadvantage to start with. No doubt that was deliberate too.

'You already know my name,' she said coolly, 'but I still don't know yours.'

'Terje,' he responded. 'You're already aware of the rest, of course.' He paused, as if waiting for something from her, lifting an eyebrow when she failed to make any comment. 'So are you going to tell me why you're here?'

'I'd have thought it obvious,' she said. 'I came to try and sort out our family affairs. Sixty years is a long time to keep up a rift. My grandmother paid all her life for daring to love an Englishman rather than one of her own countrymen, but surely these are more enlightened times?'

There was no telling his immediate reaction to the impassioned little speech. He simply continued to study her as if she were some object of curiosity for a moment or two.

'Why now?' he asked at length. 'As you said, it's a long time.'

'This isn't the first approach from our side. My father tried to make contact when his mother died more than twelve years ago.'

'And received no reply?'

'If he had, I probably wouldn't be here now.' She paused to choose her words. 'The only reason I'm here at all is because I'm the last of the Harley line. Once the name is gone, the link is gone too. I think it would be shameful to allow that to happen without someone making an effort to put things right.'

'Your father is still alive?'

'Yes.'

'But he didn't see fit to try again?'

Green eyes met blue without flinching. 'He's always been afraid that you might think he was trying to make some kind of claim.'

He took her meaning immediately, mouth twisting. 'So he sends his daughter as emissary instead.'

'He doesn't even know I'm here,' she defended. 'This was my own idea.'

The irony remained. 'And you're not afraid of what might be thought?'

'No,' she said flatly. 'The Harleys might not have made it as far up the ladder of success, but we've never been on the begging line either. All I want is recognition for him.'

'*Only* for him?'

'Primarily,' she corrected. 'My Norwegian blood is rather more diluted than his. I inherited my mother's colouring.'

'So I see.' His tone was dry. 'English all the way through!'

'And proud of it!' She made no attempt to mute the acridity. 'I don't pretend to feel any particular affinity with the Brulands as a whole. I know too little about you.'

'But you want to know more?'

'Yes, I do. If only to try and understand the mentality of a people who would disown their own daughter for such a reason.' She paused, then added with deliberation, 'Or was there perhaps more to it than just a general aversion to the English?'

'About that I wouldn't know.' His tone had hardened again. 'I doubt if it would serve any good purpose if the link were restored. We can have little in common.'

'I think that should be for your father to decide, if anyone,' Kirsten returned determinedly. 'Assuming he's now head of the family?'

He contemplated her in silence for a moment, lean features set, then he straightened abruptly away from the desk-edge to reach for the telephone. She studied the broad-shouldered, lean-hipped outline as he dialled a number, remembering the way he had looked in close-fitting jeans. So different now, yet just as stomach-curling. A man any woman with normal responses would find physically attractive, she was bound to acknowledge.

It was his manner she didn't care for. That hadn't altered at all. She wondered if he regarded all women with the same contempt he had displayed the other night. That might explain why he was still unmarried.

And what made her so sure he *wasn't* married? came the

thought. Comparatively few men took it on themselves to wear a ring. It might not be a custom at all in Norway, if it came to that. For all she really knew, he not only had a wife, but several children into the bargain.

He was speaking rapidly on the telephone—too fast once again for her to pick out any recognisable word, apart from the name of Harley itself.

'That was my father,' he said when he replaced the receiver. 'He wants to see you.'

'To say what?' she asked.

'You'll find that out when you meet him.' Expression controlled, he added, 'I'll take you through.'

There was nothing certain even now, Kirsten warned herself as she accompanied him from the office. If Leif Bruland was anything like his son, it was doubtful if any real harmony could ever be established. But at least she would have tried.

Their progression through the busy concourse drew speculative interest from all sides. Kirsten kept her gaze fixed firmly forwards, aware with every fibre of the tall, lithe figure striding at her side. There probably wasn't a female present who wasn't equally aware of his vital masculinity. Terje Bruland—several times removed, perhaps, but still a cousin. She couldn't bring herself to accept it.

Unlike in many British companies where the higher ranks tended to be separated from general staff, the Bruland hierarchy apparently preferred to be part and parcel. The chairman's personal secretary had a desk outside his office door, partitioned from the rest only by a waist-high screen, while the door itself stood ajar as if inviting entry by anyone with a mind to confer.

At first glance, Leif Bruland appeared no more welcoming than his son had been. Apart from the difference in age, the physical resemblance was marked. Two men of like stature, blue-eyed, blond-haired and tanned by outdoor activity. Only on closer approach was it possible to see the hint of silver at the older man's temples. Mid-fifties, Kirsten guessed.

'Hello,' she greeted him before he could speak. *'Hvordan står det til?'*

His brows lifted, and a smile touched his lips. *'Bare bra takk. Og med dig?'*

'Bra, takk.' She spread her hands in a wryly humorous gesture. 'That's about my conversational limit, I'm afraid, although I can understand a few words more.'

'A worthy effort,' Leif applauded. 'More than I would have expected.'

His accent was much more pronounced than his son's, Kirsten noted, though he seemed to have as little difficulty in switching languages. She gave him a tentative smile.

'I'd be the first to admit that the English aren't renowned for their linguistic abilities.'

'It's nothing to be proud of,' observed Terje drily.

'I know,' she agreed without looking at him. 'Sheer laziness on the whole.'

'Or lack of incentive due to the fact that so many other nationalities have English as their second tongue,' put in the older man. His manner this time was less restrained. 'Will you have a seat? It seems we have much to discuss.'

She sat down in the nearest chair, irritated once more when Terje remained standing by the window. She wished he would leave her to talk to his father alone, but it was hardly likely that he would. At what point, she wondered, would he bring in the fact that they had met on board ship? The telephone conversation had hardly been long enough to cover such detail. More to the point, what exactly would he say about that meeting? She would hate to have Leif Bruland regard her in the same light as did his son.

Another matter that would have to be tackled if and when it arose, she decided. Terje might be as reluctant as she was to have the circumstances known.

'I'm sorry to drop on you like this without warning,' she said. 'I'd have written first, except. . .'

'Except for the conviction that we wouldn't bother to reply,' Terje finished for her as she hesitated. 'It seems there was some attempt to renew acquaintance a number of years ago.'

'Not *seems*,' she said firmly, '*was*. And yes, I suppose that was the main reason why I didn't write first.'

'It would have been my father who chose not to make reply,' said Leif on a wry note. 'He is very much of the old school.'

'He's still alive?' Kirsten queried, not sure whether he had used the right tense.

'Very much so, although over eighty in years now.'

'So he would have been in his twenties when my grandmother was banished.'

His brows drew together. 'So it appears. I know few details of the event myself. Only that she was taken away by an Englishman named Harley.'

'Not taken away,' Kirsten insisted, 'driven!'

'That can only be hearsay,' put in Terje brusquely. 'Why should one version of the story be any more believable than the other?'

'Because mine is borne out by the fact that your grandfather refused even to acknowledge her death,' she flashed back. 'She was cast out because she fell in love with a non-Norwegian!'

'Is it of relevance after all this time?' asked Leif on a mild note. 'If we're to close the breach at all, then the past must be put aside.'

He was right, of course, Kirsten acknowledged ruefully.

She was supposedly here with an olive-branch, not a sword. 'My father will be delighted to know you're ready to recognise the relationship,' she said. 'He's wanted it for so long.'

'These are more enlightened times,' Terje reminded her mockingly. 'What other course could we take?'

His father looked from one to the other with an odd expression, as if recognising a discord greater than the situation seemed to call for. 'Where are you staying?' he asked.

'The Rosenkrantz. At least for the next few days. There's so much I want to see while I'm here,' she added. 'I thought of going up to Trondheim. That's where my grandmother was born, isn't it?'

'It's where the family originated,' Leif confirmed. 'We have a branch of the family also in Oslo. You should meet them too.'

Kirsten smiled and shook her head. 'It would be nice, of course, but I'm limited for time. I'll have to fly up to Trondheim as it is. It would take too long by road.'

'Terje flies his own plane. He will take you.' He gave her no chance to refute this suggestion. 'In the meantime, you must stay with us, of course.'

'That isn't necessary,' she protested, temporarily shelving the previous offer. 'I'm quite comfortable at the hotel.'

'And what kind of people would we be if we allowed a member of the family to stay in a hotel?' Leif shook his head decisively. 'If Terje has nothing pressing—' with an enquiring glance at his son '–he can take you back there now to collect your belongings and then out to the house.'

'What could be pressing after three weeks away?' came the satirical comment from the window.

To make any further protest would be like slapping Leif in the face, Kirsten conceded wryly. It was more than ob-

vious that Terje didn't care for the idea, although as he was
unlikely to be living in the same house as his parents she
failed to see why it should matter to him anyway.

'What about your wife?' she asked Leif. 'Will she mind
having an unexpected guest?'

'My wife was killed in a skiing accident two years ago,'
he replied unemotionally. 'I'll telephone the housekeeper
to prepare a room for you.'

'I'm so sorry.' She hardly knew what else to say. 'It's
very kind of you to go to all this trouble.'

'A family commitment,' said Terje, moving away from
the window at last. 'Shall we go?'

'I will see you later,' promised Leif as she came somewhat reluctantly to her feet. 'We still have a great deal to
talk about.' His smile was reassuring. '*Velkommen, kusine.*'

'*Tusentakk*,' she responded gratefully.

There was the gauntlet to run again back to the lift. Terje
was silent all the way down to the ground floor, urging her
out ahead of him with a curt gesture. The reception clerk
was missing from his post, but the security guard showed
enough interest for two. If the grapevine here were anything
like those at home, Kirsten thought, rumour would be rife
already, with several variations on the theme of who and
what and why.

'I didn't intend this,' she said diffidently when they were
outside the building.

'What else would you have expected?' His tone was
short.

'To be honest, I hadn't planned beyond the initial con-
frontation,' she confessed. 'I know that must sound odd,
but it's the truth. I never really expected it to be so easy.'

'If it were up to me alone, it wouldn't have been,' came
the unmoved response. 'You'd better be prepared to behave
responsibly while you're here.'

CHAPTER THREE

PAUSING at a silver-grey Mercedes parked in a slot close by the main entrance, Terje opened the passenger door and stood waiting for Kirsten to get in.

'If that remark was in reference to the other night, I'm not the only one needing to think about responsible behaviour!' she clipped 'What you did—'

'What I did was a great deal less than you invited me to do.' The fleeting smile was humourless. 'A great deal less than I was moved to do, if the truth were known. You're a very attractive young woman–with a body any man with normal instincts would lust after. My instincts are very normal.'

There was nothing flattering in the comment. She said coolly, 'Am I supposed to thank you for containing yourself?'

'No,' he replied. 'Just to remember where enticement of that nature might lead.'

'Men being the animals they are, you mean!'

His lip curled. 'Had I been an animal, you would have known it.'

It was beyond her to keep this up, Kirsten acknowledged ruefully. She clamped down hard on the sudden urge to tell him how unlike her normal behaviour the other night had been. Not only would he be unlikely to believe her, but she would also be intimating that his opinion was of importance to her.

'Are you going to get in the car?' he asked.

Fuming, she did so. He closed the door quietly, and came round to slide his length behind the wheel, firing the ignition with a flick of a lean brown wrist. Roomy as the luxurious saloon was, Kirsten still felt confined.

'I suppose you have your own home,' she said as they reached the road, determined not to allow him to see her discomfited. 'Any children?'

'I'm not married.' After a moment he glanced her way. 'Did you say something?'

If they were into straight talking, why not make it wholesale? she thought recklessly. 'I said it figures. Is it women in general you hold a grudge against, or Englishwomen in particular?'

Just for a moment his jaw seemed to tense, then he laughed drily. 'I'd find a world devoid of your sex very dull.'

'Oh, I'm sure we have our uses.' Her tone was saccharine-sweet. 'After all, you have your natural instincts to satisfy!'

'Lust isn't confined to the male,' he said. 'But I don't need to tell *you* that.'

She drew in a sharp breath. 'I made a bit of a gesture, that was all!'

'A gesture designed to provoke a response.'

'Not the kind you mean!'

'You're saying that all you wanted was a romantic kiss in the moonlight?'

The irony made her wince; it was so close to the truth. 'Did you never do something on the spur of the moment that was totally out of character?' she asked, low-toned.

'People don't act out of character,' he returned unequivocally. 'You made your interests obvious from the beginning.'

'How?' she demanded with rising heat.

'First of all by holding back until everyone else had boarded—until I had no choice but to help you with your suitcase—and then again in the cafeteria when you chose to sit at my table.'

'There was nowhere else to sit,' she said between her teeth. 'I didn't even see you there until after I sat down!'

'And the provocative conversation,' he continued as if she hadn't spoken.

She bit her lip in recollection. 'To which you contributed,' she defended.

'True,' he agreed. 'It passed the time.'

They had reached the bridge across the fjord. Looking out on the busy dockland scene, Kirsten could hardly believe that less than an hour had gone by since she had last passed this way. If she had had even an inkling of what she was going to find, she might well have decided not to bother.

'And I knew you were going to be on deck at two o'clock in the morning too, of course?' she suggested caustically.

'No, that was obviously pure chance.' Terje followed the road round to the left, skirting the dockside. 'Tell me, how far would you have allowed this. . .gesture of yours to go if I'd answered you the way you anticipated?'

The hurt of it caught her by the throat. For a brief moment she was tempted to rake her nails down the lean, uncaring cheek turned to her. 'You must consider yourself irresistible!' she declared weakly.

The sarcasm failed to touch him. 'For some women the instrument is unimportant.'

'Oh, I see. Not so much the singer but the song itself!'

'That is one way of putting it.' He sounded suddenly amused. 'An interesting turn of phrase.'

'It happens to be *my* language,' she responded shortly. 'I'm not going to defend myself against a cynic like you over a simple teasing impulse!'

'Just make sure you have no further impulses while you're staying with us,' he advised. 'Another time I might not feel like drawing back.'

The implication in the word 'us' took sudden precedence over anger. 'You still share a home with your father?'

'And his father too.' He gave her a quizzical glance. 'You find it odd that three generations of men should live together?'

'I'd have thought you'd prefer a place of your own at your age.'

'And what age is that?'

She hesitated. 'Thirty-two?'

'Close,' he said. 'I'm thirty-three. I see no need as yet of a home of my own.' There was no element of defensiveness in his tone. 'We each have our own rooms where we can be alone if we want to be.'

'And if you marry—would your wife be expected to share the same accommodation?'

'That,' he said, 'will be entirely her choice.'

Will, not would, Kirsten reflected. That seemed to suggest an arrangement already made. Whoever she was, the woman must be something special to satisfy Terje Bruland's exacting standards. Good luck to her!

They had come out on to the Strandkaien backing the waterfront where the flower-sellers were spread. A lovely, lively scene lit by a sun now high in the sky. A lone Scottish piper, resplendent in full ceremonial dress, played to a gathered crowd of onlookers, a case open at his feet to receive any appreciative offerings. Above and beyond rose the encircling mountains, pine-clad peaks misted by rising heat.

'Is summer always as good as this?' she asked in an effort to put the conversation on a more general level. 'It being on the same latitude as Alaska, I expected it to be much cooler.'

'We are having an unusual run of fine weather at present,' Terje confirmed. 'Hardly any rain at all in the past week, I'm told. We have the gulf stream to thank for the temperate climate. The winters here in Bergen itself are rarely severe, although we don't have to go far to find harsher conditions, of course.'

'I imagine you do a lot of skiing?'

'Whenever possible.' He sounded almost affable. 'Do you ski yourself?'

'All year round,' she claimed.

'Dry slopes? Hardly the same thing.'

'I've also skied in Austria and Switzerland,' she returned with some asperity. 'That's surely on a par with anything you have here?'

'You're speaking of a vacation; here it's a way of life. The ski was invented by Norwegians; did you know that?'

She shook her head 'I'll take your word for it.'

'*Takk.*' His tone was dry. Rounding the head of the harbour, he took the steeply sloping street opposite. 'The Fløyen funicular terminal is at the top here,' he announced before turning left on to Rosenkrantz. 'A view you shouldn't miss.'

'As a matter of fact, I'd intended going up there this afternoon,' she admitted. 'I wasn't lying when I said I didn't expect to be invited to stay. From what I've read about you people, you don't do a lot of home entertaining.'

'We prefer to confine it to family and very close friends, yes. As a cousin—even a remote one—you have some claim to hospitality.'

'But you wouldn't have issued the invitation yourself,

even if you'd been prepared to accept the relationship in the first place?' she challenged.

They had come to a stop outside the hotel. Terje switched off the engine, lifting his shoulders in a brief but telling shrug. 'What *I* would or wouldn't have done is immaterial. It will save a lot of time if you go up and start packing while I explain matters at the desk.'

It made sense, Kirsten supposed, although she objected to the intimation that she was incapable of handling the matter herself. She preceded him into the lobby, heading for the lift without a backward glance. He could wait where he was for as long as it took. She didn't intend hurrying either.

Apart from the remade bed, the room was as she had left it. She took her suitcase from the upper cupboard where she had stored it out of the way, and laid it open on the bed before beginning to gather her things together. Given a choice, she would have preferred to stay on here, but Leif had left her with none. He had met her more than halfway, she had to admit, yet she still felt an intruder. Terje's fault, not his father's. Apart from taking her to his father in the first place instead of simply showing her the door, he was making no concessions. He liked her no more than she liked him.

She could live with it, she told herself resolutely. It wasn't going to be for long. She had done what she had set out to do and made contact, that was the most important thing.

The patriarch of the family might well prove the biggest hurdle. A follower of the old school of thought, Leif had said, which didn't hold out a great deal of hope for a friendly welcome. At twenty odd years of age he would have been old enough to remember her grandmother with clarity–always providing he could remember anything at all. At eighty plus, he might even be senile.

She was refilling her toilet bag in the bathroom when the knock came on the door. A porter to take her bag down, she surmised, going to open it.

Terje seemed to fill the whole doorway, not so much with bulk as with sheer presence. 'I thought you might need help out to the lift,' he said. 'Unless you gained in strength over the last couple of days?'

'Supposing we just agree to forget the whole episode?' Kirsten suggested, trying not to sound too concerned either way. 'As you obviously didn't tell your father that we already met on the boat, you're none to proud of your side of it either.'

The blue eyes took on a new and indecipherable expression as he studied her. 'I agree that walking away would have been the better policy,' he said, 'but it wasn't shame that kept me from telling him. It just didn't seem relevant. Are you ready to leave?'

He wasn't prepared to meet her even a quarter of the way, she concluded. Well, fine with her! Chin tilting, she turned back into the room. 'I'll be a few minutes yet,' she tossed over a shoulder. 'And I can manage thanks!'

'I'll wait,' he said.

Tossing the toilet bag on top of the neatly folded clothing with scant regard, she closed down the lid of the case and snapped the locks. Terje moved forward to lift it easily from the bed as she reached for her jacket and shoulder-bag, indicating that she should precede him from the room.

He said nothing at all going down in the lift. Kirsten had the feeling that he was bored with the whole affair. He wasn't on his own there either. If it weren't for Leif, there would be little point in taking things any further. So far as Terje himself was concerned, she simply wasn't welcome.

'I think it might be a better idea if I spent the day doing as I first planned, and came out to the house later by taxi,' she said when they reached the lobby. 'I'm keen to visit Fløyen, and you must have a lot to catch up on after three weeks away.'

He considered her for a moment as if weighing up the odds, then glanced at his watch and came to some obvious, if not particularly ready decision. 'Nothing that can't wait another day. It's lunchtime now. We'll eat first, then take the funicular.'

'I meant alone.'

'That's unfortunate.' He sounded unmoved. 'It will be better to go to the house later, when Rune will be fresh from his afternoon rest.'

'You call your grandfather by his first name?' she asked, momentarily distracted.

'He prefers it that way.' A brief smile touched the firm mouth. 'Bestefar makes him feel old.' He nodded towards the desk where several people were in the process of checking in. 'Don't forget to leave your key.'

She went to do so, regretting now that she had made the suggestion. The thought of spending the whole afternoon in Terje's company was off-putting, to say the least. They were two people at total odds with one another.

But you're not unaware of him as a man, came the sneaking little voice, bringing a sudden tightness to her chest. Basic chemistry, she told herself. No more than that.

He was gone when she turned. She went out through the main doors to see him putting her suitcase into the boot of the car he had left parked a short distance down the road. He signalled her to stay where she was.

'We may as well eat here,' he said on return. 'Then we only have to go around the corner to reach the funicular terminal.'

'I'm not really hungry,' Kirsten denied, and saw his lips twist.

'But I am. As I told you before, we breed healthy appetites. You can choose as much or as little as you want from a *koldtbord*.'

Short of refusing point-blank to accompany him, she had little other choice, she thought wryly. He had taken over completely.

It was only just midday, but the hotel restaurant was already well populated. From the snatches of conversation overheard as they made their way to a free table at the rear of the room, Kirsten judged that the clientele consisted mostly of tourists. Not one of Terje's regular haunts, she imagined.

Hungry or not, the *koldtbord* whetted her appetite. More elaborate than the one on board ship, the number and variety of dishes on offer was amazing: marinated and smoked herring, cold salmon, trout and halibut in aspic, seafood in abundance. There were also cold cuts of meat, pâtés, hot sausages and meatballs, to say nothing of the various egg dishes and salads, fruit, bread and cheese.

'Start with the fish,' Terje advised, as the American in front of him piled everything on to the one plate. 'You can come back as many times as you like.'

Kirsten took a portion of the smoked herring, and returned to her seat, waiting until Terje joined her before picking up her cutlery. His plate held little more than her own, she saw in surprise.

'The point is to enjoy the meal at a leisurely pace,' he said, reading her thoughts. 'A fresh plate for each different dish. We normally drink *akevitt* or beer with *koldtbord*, but perhaps you would prefer wine for yourself?'

She shook her head. 'I'll have the *akevitt*, please. I tried some last night on board ship. It. . .'

She broke off, seeing the mocking tilt of an eyebrow and recalling her own request to forget the whole episode. Any reference to the voyage here, no matter how innocuous, was obviously going to elicit the same response. Trust him to take it to extremes! 'It was very good,' she finished defiantly.

He called a waiter over and ordered for them both, the *akevitt* her for, the beer, she assumed, for himself. She stole a glance at him as he turned his attention to his plate, registering the crisp cleanliness of the thick sun-kissed hair. Wonderful to run one's fingers through, came the unbidden thought, tensing muscle and sinew once again. This had to stop, she told herself fiercely. She couldn't afford to allow his physical attraction to take any hold on her.

She chose the cured meat called *spekemat* on her second trip to the buffet table, teaming it at Terje's advice with scrambled eggs and several of the paper-thin barley and rye crackers known as *flatbrød*. A delicious combination, she had to admit, on taking her first bite. Flavoured with caraway seeds and spices, the ice-cold potato brandy was the perfect accompaniment.

Terje aside, things had worked out better than she had ever really anticipated. The whole idea had been a gamble from its inception. To be able to return to her father with the news that relations had been, if not exactly cemented, at least restored, was all she wanted. It would bring him such pleasure.

There was mustard on the table; two different kinds. She reached for the nearest.

'That's Norwegian, and sweet,' said Terje. 'You'll need the French kind if you like it hot and spicy.'

French mustard—*fransk sennep*. Her head jerked, eyes meeting his involuntarily, seeing the derisive glint in sudden searing anger. If that was the way he wanted to play it, then to hell with his admonitions. She would give as good as she got!

Her smile was slow and deliberated. 'What else?'

The vivid depths of his eyes drew her in, held her gaze inexorably. She lifted her glass in taunting salute. '*Lykke til*!'

He made no verbal answer, just continued to regard her with that same contemplative expression for a moment or two, then he gave a dismissive shrug and went back to eating, leaving her feeling less than proud of herself for having given way to the retaliatory impulse. If they were going to be living under the same roof for the next few days, then she would have to acquire some necessary detachment.

It was hot enough when they got outside to make any kind of formal dress uncomfortable. Terje removed both jacket and tie and slung them on to the back seat of the car, then rolled the sleeves of his pristine white shirt to his elbows.

'You had better change your shoes,' he advised, with a glance at Kirsten's none too practical high heels. 'We don't want any accidents.'

He opened up the boot, waiting with outward patience while she located a pair of comfortable sandals. With her suit jacket removed, the short-sleeved tan blouse and cream skirt felt casual enough. Sunbathing in a sheltered spot on the upper deck yesterday had topped up her winter tan, although it came nowhere near Terje's in depth.

Leaning there against the side of the car, he was redolent of fitness and health, every muscle primed to peak condition. She had always prided herself on her own level of fitness, but he made her feel inadequate.

Covered in creeper, with a wide arched doorway and windows, the funicular station looked more like a private house. A tunnel sloped down from the payment kiosk just inside the doorway to tall iron gates, beyond which another tunnel rose almost perpendicularly. There was a small crowd of people already waiting, and, judging from the rumbling sounds echoing from the tunnel, a car fast approaching.

The gates remained closed until the car had come to rest between the two sets of steep stone steps. Descending passengers emerged from the right, leaving the ascending ones to file in from the left. Terje urged Kirsten into the lower of the stepped compartments, choosing seats to the rear so that they were facing the drop rather than the rise.

'You get the best view this way,' he said.

Her stomach lurched as the car began to lift at a steep angle. She had no particular fear of heights, but anything of this nature always called up memories of a film she had seen where a cable car became stuck hundreds of feet in the air above a mountainside, with the cables threatening to snap any minute. Funiculars were different, though, in that they stayed with the ground.

'It's perfectly safe,' Terje assured her, sensing her tension, slight though it was. 'We never lost a passenger yet.'

'I'm fine,' she said, feeling foolish. 'Really.'

Constricted by the need to make room for three other people occupying the same bench seating, they were thigh to thigh. She could feel the firm muscle through two thicknesses of material, stirring her senses afresh. Whatever detachment she managed to achieve, it could only be of the mind, not the body, she acknowledged. No amount of objectivity could rid her of this physical awareness.

They left the darkness of the tunnel and rose at a steep angle through the trees, stopping twice at stations used like bus stops by those who lived on the higher levels of the zig-zagging streets. Terje led the way up the steep flight of steps when they finally alighted from the car at the upper terminal, to emerge through a turnstile on to a wide fenced path and a view that was every bit what Kirsten had anticipated.

The whole city was spread out below like a relief map; a pattern of peaking gables and mellow red-tiled roofs broken here and there by domes and spires of copper turned green with verdigris. An octagonal lake with a fountain spouting at its centre occupied the foreground. From there, the eye was drawn up and out via the pointing finger of land which formed the inner harbour, to the wide blue waters of the fjord with its backcloth of islands, sea and sky.

'I imagine you could come up here every day and never find it boring!' she exclaimed with genuine enthusiasm, forgetting hostilities for the moment. 'There's so much to look at! I think I can even pick out your premises way over there. The big white block with the flag mast on top?'

'There's obviously nothing wrong with your eyesight,' Terje responded, intimating that it was about the only thing he found right with her. 'That's Brulands, yes. One of the best times to be up here is at sunset. Unfortunately, at this time of year it has to be shared with a horde of tourists.

'Who all bring in revenue to the city.' She kept her tone light. 'One of the crosses you have to bear—although I shouldn't have said tolerance was one of your strong points.'

He glanced her way, taking in the emerald sparkle of her eyes, the fresh colour in her face. Something seemed to harden in him. 'It depends on what I'm called upon to be tolerant of. Where you're concerned, I'm fighting a losing battle.'

'Reciprocated!' she flashed back, abandoning all prospect of detachment. 'You know, if it weren't for my father, I'd say to hell with the whole thing!'

There was no hint of apology in the lean features. 'If it were not for our respective fathers, and their fathers before them, we'd neither of us be standing here at all. I accept the relationship, but that, where I'm concerned, is as far as it goes. If my father wants to further it himself, that is his affair. Shall we move on?' he added with scarcely a pause. 'You didn't get to see the whole scene yet.'

Kirsten braced herself against the almost overwhelming desire to lash out as he turned away. The best way to deal with him would be to allow everything he said to simply wash over her head, but she wasn't capable of that. It hurt to be regarded with such aversion. If it hadn't been for that incident on board ship, they might have found some level of communication, but not now. His whole attitude towards her was inflexible.

The city was bigger than she had thought, spreading southwards in an elongated wedge between fjord and mountains. The composer, Edvard Grieg, had lived out there by the Nordas lake, Terje told her. His ashes, and those of his wife Nina, were entombed in the grounds of the house, which was now a museum.

'You should take the opportunity to visit Troldhaugen while you're staying with us,' he said. 'We live within a ten-minute walk. Are you familiar with Grieg's music at all?'

Kirsten resisted the impulse to say she preferred pop to classical; it would have been both childish and untrue. 'I think most people would be familiar with *Peer Gynt* and *Holberg*,' she returned, 'if only in part. I like his vocal works myself.'

He gave her a swift glance. 'Do you sing?'

She laughed and shook her head. 'Only in the shower. I was sorry to have missed the International Festival. May, wasn't it?'

'Yes.' For once the blue eyes held a spark of interest. 'The Bergen Philharmonic season is over, but there are recitals at Troldhaugen through the summer months.'

'Terje!' Spoken in tones of sharp surprise, the name drew them both about to face the young woman who had just detached herself from a passing tour group. She rested a brief glance on Kirsten, then looked back to the man at her side, addressing him in Norwegian with a questioning inflexion.

He answered in the same language, with Kirsten Harley, *kusine* and England the only recognisable words; switching to English to add, 'I would like you to meet Inger Torvund. Kirsten has no Norwegian, Inger.'

The latter's smile was perfunctory. 'Then we will speak in English, of course. Welcome to Norway.'

Kirsten returned the smile and a 'Thank you', reluctant to try out even the few words she did know after what Terje had said. The newcomer was perhaps a year or so older than herself, with mid-length hair a shade or two darker than Terje's. She was blue-eyed too, although their paleness detracted a little from an otherwise strikingly attractive face.

'Inger is also a cousin,' Terje continued. 'Although only by marriage. My aunt became her father's second wife some few years ago.'

The parameters were spreading, Kirsten reflected. Not that she and Inger were even remotely connected. From the way she looked at Terje, it was only too easy to deduce where her interests lay. So far as Terje himself was concerned there was no knowing, although his greeting had seemed casual enough.

'I have to go,' said Inger with obvious reluctance. 'My group is waiting. Will you be staying in Bergen for very long?'

'Just a few days,' Kirsten acknowledged, and saw a flash of something very much like relief in the other eyes.

'Then we must see that you enjoy it. You must hold a family gathering one evening, Terje, so that we can all of us meet our English cousin.'

'Perhaps.' He sounded a little abrupt. '*Hils til tante Hanna.*'

Kirsten watched the girl move off to rejoin the sizeable group of people now crowding the view platform a little further along. Slim and shapely in her neat shirtwaister dress, she moved with the same lithe tread that Terje displayed.

'Inger conducts guided tours about the city,' he said, as if in some doubt of her ability to work that one out for herself. 'She speaks French and German too.'

'Good for her.' Kirsten made certain there was no trace of sarcasm in her voice. 'What does she do in the winter?'

'She teaches.'

'Obviously very clever.' She hadn't meant to say it, but the words formed themselves. 'Are you and she. . .involved?'

The glance he turned her way was too shrewd for comfort. 'Why the interest?'

'Just curious,' she said lightly. 'She's very attractive.'

'You think that's all a man looks for in a woman?'

'I suppose it depends on *why* he's looking. Short term or long term. Some men can't handle commitment.'

'That sounds like the voice of experience.'

She caught herself up, summoning a laugh. 'Too many magazine articles!' Making a show of looking at her watch, she added, 'It's gone half-past three. What will your father think if he arrives home before we get there?'

'That I took advantage of the opportunity to show you some of the city sights—what else?' If there had been any

ame site as the original, but only some thirty years

urned to look at him, steeling herself against the
f his regard. 'How much do you know about her?'
t from the fact that she went away with an English
ot a great deal,' he admitted. 'Rune could tell you
ut I doubt very much that you could persuade him
bout her even if you could speak the language. You
reaction just now when I told him who you were.'
think his attitude justified?'

road shoulders lifted briefly. 'He's an old man, with
.'

not on his own,' she retorted. 'Who is it I remind
Terje?'

scle jerked faintly in the firm jawline. 'What makes
k you remind me of anyone?'

way you've acted ever since we first met.'

was a hint of cruelty in the curl of his lip. 'You
failure to make the approach you were anticipat-

anticipating nothing,' she denied. 'Until you al-
pped your pack on my foot, I hadn't even noticed
e made an effort to re-pitch her voice, aware of its
flexion. 'I'm sure in your position you're accus-
having women throw themselves at you, but you
cold—with or without the beard!'

t so?' he said softly.

fused to back away as he moved towards her, or
gle when he pulled her to him. Instead she at-
to stay passive beneath the demanding pressure of
o disregard the clamouring urge to respond. Only
possible. The emotions he excited in her were too
ming.

nsed the change in him when she began to answer.

easing of attitude at all it wasn't showing now. He added
shortly, 'You're going to find Rune a great less welcoming
than my father. He speaks only Norwegian, for one thing.'

'Then it's lucky that I have the two of you to translate
for me,' she said, refusing to be intimidated by the thought
of meeting the old man.

There was a car already standing in when they reached
the terminal. Inger's group was milling around in the gift
shop, while Inger herself waited outside.

'We should be taking this car too,' she acknowledged,
'but we will have to wait for the next one. They refuse to
leave without their souvenirs!'

'You must have a lot of patience,' Kirsten remarked
lightly. 'I hope to see you again before I leave, but in case
I don't it was nice meeting you, Inger.'

Terje lingered behind for a private word with the girl,
causing Kirsten to wonder once again if there was more
than immediately met the eye to their relationship. The absence of intimacy from their greeting a few minutes ago
didn't necessarily mean that it didn't exist. For all she
knew, Norwegians preferred to keep their more personal
emotions to themselves.

They were the last through the barrier before it closed,
and took seats in the uppermost compartment. Unrestrained
this time by the pressure of bodies to either side, Kirsten
found herself sliding on the smooth plastic as the car began
its steep descent, and had to hold on hard to keep from
coming up against Terje, who was by the window.

Touching or not, she was vibrantly conscious of him. She
only wished she weren't. Dislike was no barrier against
physical desire—and that was what he aroused in her. She
had known it all along.

CHAPTER FOUR

SITED WITHIN its own grounds on the Nordas lake, the Bruland home was an extensive two storeys of white-painted
timbers topped by a roof of green pantiles. It was traditional
inside as well as out, with lovely glowing wood floors and
colourful rugs. Bright paintings and handwoven hangings
decorated the walls of the wide and welcoming hallway.

The woman who greeted them was in her late fifties, her
greying fair hair parted in the centre and twisted into neat
coils over her ears. Terje introduced her as Berta Gustav-
sen, the housekeeper. She spoke little English, and was reticent in her acknowledgement of Kirsten's attempt at Norwegian.

They found Rune Bruland seated beside a blazing log
fire in the big, comfortably furnished sitting-room.
Shrunken in stature from the man he must once have been,
and with features lined like a map, he was still in full possession of all his faculties, Kirsten realised when he turned
his faded blue gaze on her after Terje finished telling him
who she was. There was no warmth in his scrutiny.

She made an effort to instil some real feeling into the
only phrase she knew. Rune simply looked at her as if to
say she could see for herself how he was, then turned back
to his contemplation of the fire.

'I'll take you up to your room,' said Terje, making no
attempt to excuse his grandparent's discourtesy. 'We eat
dinner at six. Early by your standards, but—'

'When in Rome,' she finished for
to adjust my habits. What time will y

'When he arrives.'

She paused at the foot of the ope
keep her tone even. 'Is is really neces
Your father invited me here.'

'You gave him no option,' came th

'That isn't true. I was perfectly wi
was at the hotel. You cancelled the res
must know I was booked to stay the f

'In the knowledge that at this time
be no problem in re-letting the room.'

She gazed at him impotently, sear
in the armour. His antagonism stemme
meeting—no, from his very first sight
visualise that narrowed appraisal. He
then who she was.

He turned away to mount the stairs,
option but to follow. Furnished in S
carpeted in dark blue, the room to
was at the rear of the house.

'The bathroom you will be using
depositing her suitcase on a covered
the double bed. 'No guest *en suite*, I
do have a sauna along the corridor.'

'I never expected hotel facilities,
'This is lovely, thank you.'

She went to the window, looking
and trees, with glimpses of the l
Mountains ringed the horizon. So
she thought.

'Was this my grandmother's hor
'The house isn't that old,' Terje

on the s
ago.'

She t
impact

'Apar
sailor,
more, b
to talk a
saw his

'You

The b
set idea

'He's
you of,

A mu
you thin

'The

There
mean m
ing?'

'I was
most dr
you!' Sh
rising in
tomed to
leave *me

'Is tha

She re
to strugg
tempted
his lips,
it was in
overwhel

She se

He drew her closer, mouth gentling, seeking now rather than taking, yet still retaining command. She could feel the thud of his heart against her breast, the heat from his loins.

When he slid an arm beneath her knees and lifted her she made no protest. It seemed entirely natural to be with him like this, to be carried like this; to be laid on the bed with his weight bearing down on her as he sought her mouth again. Her fingers buried themselves in the thickness of his hair, revelling in texture of it; her nostrils were filled with his masculine scent. She had waited all her life, it seemed, for this one man.

His sudden movement of thrusting himself up and away from her left her suspended in shocked immobility for a second before realisation hit her. Sanity returned like a deluge of ice-cold water as she looked into the contemptuous blue eyes.

'You were saying?' he taunted.

'You louse!' She attempted to sit up, only to be pushed flat again by the hand that clamped down on her shoulder; lying there helpless against his strength. For the moment, anger was the dominant emotion. She wanted to hammer her fists into the lean face, to wipe that cynical smile from his lips. He had deliberately played her along—made her respond to him for the sole purpose of mortifying her. Only she wasn't going to give him the pleasure of seeing her mortified.

'Feeling proud of yourself?' she flung at him. 'Why not try beating your chest like the other big apes?'

There was a hard amusement in his eyes. 'You don't learn easily, do you?' he said. 'Or is it that you want more of the same?'

'Not from *you*!' She brought one hand up in a vicious swipe aimed at his jaw, clenching her teeth as he caught her wrist in an iron-like grip. 'You're hurting me!'

He loosened his grasp but retained his hold, pressing her arm down again. 'Stop acting like an outraged virgin,' he clipped. 'You lost nothing of any value. I warned you not to goad me again.'

She was in no position to indulge in retaliation, but the stab went too deep for caution to rule. 'Is it really me you want to humiliate,' she snapped, 'or am I just the whipping boy?'

The muscles about his mouth tautened ominously. 'I've never hit a woman in my life.'

'It's just a figure of speech.' She found herself suddenly on the defensive. 'You know what I mean. Was she English too?'

He released her abruptly and got to his feet. 'This has gone far enough,' he declared.

Kirsten pushed herself upright as he moved towards the door. 'I'm right, aren't I?' she flung at his departing back. 'I'm bearing the brunt for some woman who let you down!'

He halted in mid-stride, turning to look back at her with irony in his eyes. 'Don't underestimate yourself. I found it far from easy to stop where I did just now.'

'Such strength of mind!' she mocked back instinctively, and knew an instant regret as he curled a lip and began to turn away again. 'Terje, wait a minute,' she appealed. 'Please!'

He halted, looking at her dispassionately. 'Why?'

'Because, as you said just now, this whole thing has gone far enough.' She paused, searching for the right words–if there were any right words–watching his face for even the faintest encouragement. 'I *am* right, aren't I?' she said at last, unable to find any other way. 'I do remind you of someone else?'

For a moment he looked as if he might decline to answer,

then he shrugged. 'In looks *and* in manner. Another English enticer!'

'I'm not like that!' she denied. 'Not normally, anyway.'

'No?' The mockery was back. 'Then why with me?'

She made a helpless little gesture. 'I suppose partly because of the way you treated me.'

'You're accustomed to a more flattering response, of course.'

'I'm unaccustomed to being snubbed for no good reason!' she flashed, forsaking the attempt to reach some kind of understanding. 'If you hadn't been so damned arrogant, I wouldn't have given you a second thought!'

'You're claiming that you only goaded me in retaliation for the insult to your pride?'

The tone was a goad in itself. 'Yes!'

'And just now? That was also retaliation?'

Her eyes dropped, her heart jerking painfully. 'Obviously not. But I'm sure I'm not the first to be carried away by your inimitable technique!'

He gave a short laugh. 'Inimitable by how many?'

'I don't sleep around!' She kept her voice as level as she could. 'I daresay there are men who could make the same claim without lying their heads off, but I doubt if you're one of them. In fact, I'd be willing to bet that, like most men, you can't even remember how many women you've had. If one of them turned the tables on you, then good for her!'

The silence after she finished speaking seemed to stretch forever. She forced herself to look up in the end, surprised by the lack of icy anger in the blue eyes. His regard was reflective, as if he was still considering what reply to make.

'I shouldn't have said that,' she apologised thickly. 'Only neither should you make assumptions based on nothing more than a passing resemblance to someone else.'

'More than just a passing resemblance,' he said. 'You could be sisters.'

'What happened?' she asked diffidently, and saw the cynicism increase.

'I found her in bed with another man.'

Kirsten swallowed on the sudden hard lump in her throat, recalling the utter devastation she had felt on making the same discovery—seeing once again the mixture of guilt and triumph on Barbara's face as the latter looked up to see her standing there in the doorway. Nick hadn't even bothered to make excuses. They were both free agents, he'd said. Why shouldn't he take advantage of what was on offer?

'I'm sorry,' she said huskily. 'I know what that's like.'

Terje studied her speculatively. 'You had a close relationship with the man?'

'He wanted us to live together.' Her smile was crooked. 'My mother would die of shame if I moved in with a man I wasn't married to. Like your grandfather, she doesn't believe in moving with the times.'

'She can't be so old.'

'She's sixty, Dad's sixty-three. I came along when they'd almost given up hope.' Kirsten rested her chin on her bent knees, forgetting where she was for the moment. 'There's a lot of responsibility attached to being an only child of parents who waited so long to be parents at all. I'd hate to hurt either of them for the sake of a little independence.'

Terje hadn't moved from the centre of the room, standing now with hands thrust into trouser pockets and an enigmatic expression on his face. 'You'll be leaving them on their own when you marry.'

'Well, yes, I expect so. *If* I marry.'

'Not all men are alike.'

'Not all women are alike either,' she retorted, 'but *you* don't make any allowances.' She made a sudden appealing gesture. 'We're cousins, Terje–surely we should at least try to be friends?'

His smile was faint. 'I don't think so.'

'Why not?'

'Because friendship isn't what you inspire in me. I would have thought I'd made that more than obvious just now.'

She gazed at him, heart thudding against her ribcage–wanting him with a depth of need that superseded all other considerations. He was so utterly and totally male; he set her alight the way Nick had never done.

'Do you think it's only men who feel that way?' she asked huskily. 'Or are you one of those who considers it immoral for a woman to want. . .the same things?'

'The word is sex,' he said. 'A liberated woman should not find the terminology so difficult to use.'

'If we're going to be clinical about it, the actual term is sexual intercourse!' she retorted smartly, stung by the gibe, and felt her colour rise along with the sardonic tilt of his eyebrow.

'Would you like to be clinical about it right now?'

She swallowed thickly. 'No.'

'Then I think it time we ended this conversation.'

'You didn't answer the question,' she said.

The shrug came again. 'I don't consider it immoral for a woman to want a man–providing she confines herself to one man at a time. And before you say it, I don't exclude my own sex from that basic rule either.' His tone altered. 'I'll see you at *middag*.'

Kirsten waited until he had gone from the room before making any move. She felt all churned up inside. A few minutes ago she had been ready to give herself to him without even a token struggle, and he must have been aware of it. Most men would have taken advantage of the fact.

Only not Terje Bruland. He was made of stronger stuff.

A strength of mind she had better start acquiring for herself where he was concerned before she became even more involved. There was no future in allowing herself to feel anything at all for cousin Terje.

It was half-past five by the time she had unpacked. Pulling on a cotton wrap, she went to sample the bathroom facilities, finding them on a par with those at the hotel. A warm shower went a long way towards restoring her spirits. She had at least achieved something by coming here. While the Harleys and Brulands might never realise any real family closeness, sixty years of estrangement had been set aside.

Apart from Rune, of course. He wasn't going to be an easy nut to crack. If she weren't staying here, it wouldn't really matter, but his refusal to even acknowledge her—if he kept it up—was going to make for a very uncomfortable atmosphere. The language problem made things even more difficult. How did she even begin to make an appeal to him without some form of communication? Her only hope was that Leif might be able to persuade him to lighten up a little. A nod and a smile would be enough.

Wearing a calf-length dress in navy and cream, she emerged from her room on the stroke of six, to see Leif himself coming out of a door further along the landing. He was casually clad in trousers and lightweight sweater, making her feel suddenly over-dressed. Too late now to worry about it, she decided as he approached.

'I hope you find your room comfortable?' he said.

'It couldn't be more so,' Kirsten assured him. 'I want to thank you again for inviting me to stay, Leif.' She added swiftly. 'Do you mind me calling you Leif?'

'I'm your cousin,' he said. 'What else would you call me? We very rarely use titles here, anyway.'

'Do you call your father by his first name too?' she asked as they descended the wide oipen staircase.

'We all do.' He gave her a swift glance. 'Did you meet him yet?'

'Terje told him who I was,' she acknowledged wryly, 'but he didn't seem to want to know.'

'Give him time,' Leif advised. 'He'll come round.'

'If it takes more than a few days, I'll be gone, anyway,' she said. 'Perhaps it might be best to just leave it the way it is.'

'Is it essential that you adhere so strictly to your schedule?' he asked. 'Could you not extend your time with us a little more?'

They had reached the hallway. Stifling the sudden urge to snatch at the invitation, she smiled and shook her head. 'It's the last of my holiday entitlement from work, I'm afraid, but I appreciate the suggestion.'

He accepted the refusal without demur, causing her to wonder if the offer had been anything more than a polite gesture in the first place. Leif had already proved himself willing to put the past aside, but that didn't necessarily mean that he wanted to forge any closer ties with the English branch of the family.

They found both Terje and his grandfather already seated at the table in the light and airy dining-room. The Norwegian love of colour was evidenced once again in the woven wall-hangings and warmly glowing woodwork. Everything in Norway was designed to make the most of all available light, Kirsten judged. A kind of storage against the short days and long dark nights of winter, perhaps? Not that the nights here in Bergen would be half as long as those further north, where the sun never rose at all for several months of the year.

She avoided any direct eye contact with Terje as she took

her place opposite him at Leif's invitation, only too mindful
of the afternoon's events. He was dressed casually too, the
open collar of his pale cream shirt revealing a glimpse of
bronzed chest. Stripped, he would be all lean, taut muscle
and power, came the thought, bringing a dryness to her
throat. If the few moments he had devoted to arousing her
earlier were anything to go by, his lovemaking would be
out of this world!

Seated at the head of the table, as was his right, Rune
paid her no attention at all, although he conversed with both
son and grandson throughout the meal. *Middag* was no
meal for faint appetites. They began with a home-made
asparagus soup that surpassed anything that Kirsten had
ever tasted before, followed by fried slices of veal rolled
around a stuffing of forcemeat and served with potato
dumplings and gravy, along with half a dozen other vege-
tables. Dessert was a glorious concoction of meringue and
whipped cream, topped with chocolate sauce and toasted
almonds.

Cheeses, Kirsten had already discovered, were mostly
eaten at breakfast or lunch on *smørbrød*. Not that she could
have eaten any, in any case, after that feast. The amount
of food the two younger men alone managed to put away
between them was phenomenal, and Rune wasn't all that
far behind, despite his age.

'How do you keep your weight down if you eat like this
every day?' she asked Leif. 'I don't think I'll ever be hungry again!'

He laughed. 'If you lived here yourself you'd find you
needed the extra fuel. We like to spend our leisure time in
activities.'

'Kirsten skis,' said Terje. 'Dry slopes, for the most part,
but better than nothing.'

'Beggars can't be choosers,' she rejoined with what equability she could muster. 'As a matter of interest, I also play squash on a regular basis, and take aerobics twice a week, so I don't think I can be accused of too much lazing around myself.'

'Did you ever try hiking for pleasure?' he asked. 'Or rock climbing?'

'Well, no. I don't really have the time.'

'What is this job you have?' asked Leif.

'I'm an oral hygienist.' She smiled at his expression. 'That's the reaction I usually get.'

'What made you decide to take up such a career?'

'One of my aunts is married to a dentist. He persuaded me to take the course, and gave me a job in his practice when I qualified.'

'You had no wish to become a dentist yourself?'

Kirsten smiled again. 'Too long a training, not enough dedication.'

'A pity,' remarked Terje. 'You might eventually have taken over the practice.'

'He has a son to do that,' she said. 'I'm happy enough doing what I do.'

'Do you have a special man in your life?' asked Lief casually. 'Or are you still looking for the right one?'

'There's no one special,' she acknowledged, and felt her colour rise under Terje's regard. 'I'm not looking for a husband, if that's what you mean.'

'You would prefer an unfettered relationship?'

'I suppose it would depend on circumstances,' she returned cautiously.

'Afraid of commitment, perhaps?' observed Terje.

'You should know all about that!' she shot back at him.

Rune said something short and sharp, cutting off any reply Terje might have been about to make as he answered his grandfather's obvious question. Kirsten took a firm hold on her temper, only too conscious of Leif's thoughtful regard.

'I'm sorry,' she murmured. 'That was very ill-mannered of me.'

'You were provoked,' he said. 'Terje should also apologise.'

'Of course,' responded his son. The eyes meeting hers were devoid of expression. 'It was a tasteless remark.'

Rune spoke again, answered this time by Leif. Unable to hold the blue gaze, Kirsten returned her attention to the meringue still left in her dish, wishing suddenly that she could get up and walk away from this whole situation. None of them really wanted her here. She was simply a cross to bear.

'I contacted my sister, Hanna, and invited her to meet you this evening,' said Leif. 'I asked that she bring the whole family, if they are not otherwise engaged. Her stepdaughter, Inger, is close to your own age.'

'We already met,' Kirsten acknowledged. 'She was conducting a tour group on Fløyen this afternoon. Terje was kind enough to take me up there to see the view.'

'A good idea while you were in the vicinity,' Leif approved. 'You will be here too, of course?' The last to his son. 'I know you and Nils don't have a great deal to say to one another, but this is a special occasion.'

'I'll be here.' The tone was impassive.

Kirsten said quickly, 'If you already made other arrangements. . .'

'I haven't,' he returned. 'I'm three weeks out of touch.'

'You must both have come in on the same ferry,' said Leif, as if only just realising. 'Quite a coincidence!'

'Wasn't it?' agreed his son.

Rune broke in again at that point with a remark directed at both men, necessitating a switch to Norwegian to answer him. The following discussion went on for several minutes, giving Kirsten the feeling that the old man was deliberately extending it. Considering that almost the whole dinner conversation had been conducted in English for her benefit, she could hardly blame him for claiming a little attention for himself. She was the outsider, not him.

It was a relief when they retired from the table to relax in the living-room over glasses of *akevitt* while waiting for the Torvunds to arrive. Seated in his chair at the fireside, Rune showed no sign of fatigue, although he said little. There was a television set over in a corner of the room, but Kirsten suspected that it was rarely watched. From what Terje had said, reading was the main sedentary pastime.

She stole a glance at him lounging comfortably in an armchair, allowing her eyes to linger a brief moment or two on the well-defined features. Arrogant hostility was all she had known from him to date, yet it made no difference to the way he made her feel deep down inside. The muscles of her inner thighs spasmed at the mere memory of those moments she had spent in his arms this afternoon. He had aroused a sensuality she hadn't even known herself capable of.

She realised suddenly that he was looking right back at her, and hastily averted her gaze, thankful to hear the sound of car engines outside. He was too perceptive not to know what had been going through her mind. She didn't want to see the mockery in his eyes.

Hanna Torvund was a comfortably rounded woman some five or six years younger than her brother, her husband, Georg, several years older. Both were a little reticent in their greeting, although by no means hostile.

Inger put on a show of friendliness herself, but it was only surface. It was left to her brother Nils to demonstrate any real enthusiasm, which he did with a practised charm, holding on to Kirsten's hand far longer than was strictly necessary, the almost too handsome features expression open approval.

'*Velkommen, kusine!*' he said, and then in English, 'Inger's description failed to do you full justice.' Pale blue, like his sister's, his eyes went beyond her to seek those of the man standing a short distance away, taking on a new expression. 'So much like Jean!'

'In colouring, perhaps,' came the level reply. 'You will have a beer?'

A seemingly innocuous exchange, and yet to Kirsten, at least, the air was suddenly charged. There was no doubt that this Jean was the one Terje had mentioned earlier–the English girl who had two-timed him. Was it possible, she wondered in a flash of insight, that Nils was the man she had two timed him with? Leif had intimated that the two men didn't get along. If that was the reason, small wonder!

Nils never left her side all evening. In other circumstances, she might have found his attentions flattering, but she had a feeling that the degree of interest was due as much to Terje's presence as her own. He was younger than the latter by three or four years, and of a slighter build, and his looks were appealing enough, but he left her fundamental emotions untouched.

It was obvious from the way she was with him that Inger's feelings for her cousin went far deeper than a mere family fondness. He was attentive enough in return, but there was no real spark there, Kirsten judged. Or was that simply wishful thinking? she asked herself wryly. Where Terje Bruland was concerned, who could be sure of anything?

Still full from *middag*, she was unable to do any justice at all to the *smørbrød* served for supper, but drank two cups of coffee to diminish the effects of the *akevitt* they had all drunk throughout the evening. Lethal stuff, she decided ruefully, feeling her head swim when she stood up. Not that anyone else seemed affected by it.

'You must allow me to show you the parts of Bergen that you have not yet visited,' said Nils. 'I can spend the whole day with you on Saturday.'

It was still only Thursday, Kirsten realised with a sense of shock. A bare twenty-four hours since her arrival in Norway. Just one week from tomorrow she was due to board ship again for the return home. So little time!

Nils had obviously taken her agreement for granted. He would be unaccustomed, she thought, to having his invitations turned down. It was too late now to start finding excuses. She gave him a smile.

'I'll look forward to it.'

Glancing up, she found Terje watching her from across the room, and knew a sudden and urgent desire to deny any interest in his cousin.

And why should she imagine he cared? came the following and depressing thought. By his own admission, he had some physical desire for her, but his contempt overrode it. She couldn't blame him for thinking her easy; she had done little to persuade him otherwise.

CHAPTER FIVE

It was Rune who finally brought an end to the evening by announcing himself ready to retire for the night. Kirsten had to admire the old man for his stamina, if nothing else. His refusal to accept any closure of the rift was so irrational. Whatever the feelings instilled in him at the time of his sister's departure from the family, things had come a long way since then. Surely he could at least make some small concession?

Nils arranged to pick her up on Saturday morning. Unlike Terje, he had his own apartment on Nordas Point, he advised, leaving her with the feeling that the day might include a home visit. Nothing wrong with that, of course—providing a visit was all he anticipated.

She was becoming a total cynic, she chided herself. She had no reason to suspect ulterior motives on Nils's part. He was taking her sightseeing, no more.

Leif declared himself also ready to retire after seeing the Torvunds away.

'As it's Friday tomorrow, and you have nothing vital scheduled, there is little reason for you to come in to the office, is there?' he suggested to Terje. 'Why don't you take Kirsten out to Hardangerfjord?'

'I can go alone,' she claimed hastily. 'It really isn't necessary.'

'Better to have company,' Lief responded. 'I'm sure Terje has no objection?'

'None at all,' returned the latter without particular inflexion. 'As you say, I have a free calendar. I'm going to take a walk before bed,' he added to Kirsten herself. 'Why don't you join me?'

The invitation took her by surprise. She looked at him uncertainly, trying to read the mind behind the enigmatic blue eyes. Whether he was offering her a genuine olive-branch or simply acting the part for his father's benefit was impossible to tell.

The thought of a bedtime stroll in the lovely Norwegian summer twilight was appealing enough in its own right. 'Thanks, I'd like to,' she said on what she hoped was a casual note.

'I'll leave you to it,' said Leif. 'Goodnight, Kirsten.'

'*God natt,*' she returned without even thinking about it, and saw a smile cross the older man's face as he turned to take the stairs.

There was little initial conversation. Terje seemed content to maintain a silence that was if not exactly companionable, at least lacked open hostility. Woody and bird-welcoming, the grounds stretched down to the lakeside, where there was a substantial boathouse and private jetty.

''Far likes to fish,' Terje advised. 'He sometimes spends the whole evening out on the lake at this time of the year.'

'Not a hobby of yours, though?' Kirsten hazarded.

He shook his head. 'I prefer to use a boat more actively. Do you do any sailing yourself?'

'No,' she admitted. 'Something else I never found time to try.'

'I'll take you out this weekend, if you like,' he offered, again unexpectedly. 'Saturday?'

She bit her lip. 'Could we make it Sunday instead? I'm supposed to be spending Saturday with Nils. I thought you knew.'

'I guessed he might be making some arrangement,' came the measured response. 'On Sunday we're flying up to Trondheim. It will be the only opportunity.'

Kirsten stole a glance at him, silhouetted against the nebulous skyline, registering the effect on her pulse-rate with a sense almost of despair. He looked so remote, so untouchable.

'I know I said I'd like to visit Trondheim,' she ventured, 'but it really isn't essential. I'm taking up too much of your time as it is.'

'It's my time,' he returned. 'Unless, of course, you'd prefer to spend the whole weekend with cousin Nils?'

'No!' Too quick, and too emphatic, the denial was a total give-away, she thought wryly. She made an attempt to temper it. 'I'm only spending Saturday because it would have seemed churlish to refuse.'

Even in this light, the blue eyes were penetrating. 'He doesn't interest you?'

She hesitated, aware of the pitfalls in whatever reply she made. 'I find him attractive to look at,' she said at length, 'but I'm not attracted to him.'

Terje smiled briefly. 'Only a woman could make such a distinction. For a man, the two are the same.'

'Is he the one you found with Jean?' she heard herself asking, and could have bitten off her tongue as his expression chilled again. 'Forget I said that,' she urged. 'It's none of my business.'

'But an astute guess.' His tone was short. 'Feminine instinct again?'

'I suppose you could call it that.' Kirsten let the pause stand for a second or two. 'You don't object to having him in the house?'

He shrugged. 'I don't pretend to have any regard for him, but neither do I have any reason to shun him.'

'You mean you don't consider what he did reason enough?'

'He did what most men would do in such a situation,' came the flat response. 'He took what was offered him.'

Kirsten was glad of the semi-darkness to conceal her flush at the memory of her own readiness to give herself that afternoon. Most men, perhaps.

'So no blame attached?' she said, taking refuge in sarcasm. 'How terribly unfair I was on poor Nick!'

'That would depend on the circumstances. Did you know the girl you found him with?'

'Oh, yes.' She couldn't stop the bitterness from creeping in. 'She was my supposed best friend!'

'And you think her the less culpable?'

She was silent, visualising once again the expression on Barbara's face. The latter had never tried to hide the fact that she found Nick attractive; she had even made the odd remark about stepping in if she, Kirsten, ever felt like stepping out. It had been a joke between them. Or so it had appeared.

'I suppose it was probably six of one and half a dozen of the other,' she admitted.

'Did they stay together?'

She shook her head. 'It was just the one time. They didn't even get on all that well.'

'But you didn't consider renewing the relationship?'

'Did *you*?' she retorted.

The smile was faint. 'Not for a moment.'

'So what did happen?'

'She went back home to England. More than a year ago now.'

'Gone, but not forgotten,' Kirsten said softly, and saw his lips slant again.

'She was, until two days ago.

Heart thudding, unable to look away from the mesmeric eyes, she said, 'Would you have been as much against reconciliation between our families if I hadn't given you the impression I did on board ship?'

'Not so much against as unable to see very much point,' he returned. 'There's Rune to consider. He's too old to change his way of thinking.'

'You could talk to him.'

'I could,' he agreed, 'but I won't. He's entitled to be left in peace.'

Kirsten looked away, throat tight. 'There isn't much point in my staying on, then, is there?'

'My father wants you to stay.' His voice was expressionless.

'But, like your grandfather, you'd prefer that I went?'

He made no verbal answer to that. She tensed at the touch of his hand on her arm, drawing her round to face him. His was so devastatingly virile; he made her go weak at the knees. A comma of blond hair had fallen across his forehead. She put up an involuntary hand to push it back, quivering at the expression in the vivid eyes.

His lips were compelling, inciting instant response. He drew her closer, bringing her into contact with the hard and yet so infinitely accommodating angles of his body. He was a tactile revelation, his skin taut over muscle vibrant with controlled power, his hand so supple, seeking the full firmness of her breast through the thin covering of material. She wanted to be closer still, to feel the long lean fingers caressing her bare flesh—to lose herself in sheer sensation. There was nothing more vital in the world!

There was self-respect, came the still small voice. Did she have none left at all? Terje didn't care about her; not in any way that mattered. He was simply doing what most men would do and taking what was offered. He had said it himself.

She thrust herself sharply away from him, backing off out of arm's reach. 'I think it's time to go back,' she got out.

'An eye for an eye?' he queried on a hardened note.

He was referring to this afternoon, Kirsten realised at once. He thought she had done this purposely. So why not let him go on thinking it? Better that than have him consider her his for the taking.

'Now we're all equal,' she agreed, assuming a harder note of her own.

He contemplated her narrowly for a moment, then he gave a shrug, as if deciding that the incident wasn't worth bothing about. 'You're right,' he said. 'It's time we went back.'

He had little to say on the way. Kirsten had the feeling that he had lost interest in her all the way through. Better for her if he had, she told herself, and tried to shut out the sense of desolation.

Lying between cool cotton sheets some twenty minutes later, she knew sleep was going to be a long time coming. If she hadn't come to her senses back there, she wouldn't have been able to face Terge at all in the morning, she consoled herself. She could just imagine the way he would have regarded her if she had allowed her emotions full rein.

Knowing it didn't stop her from wanting him, though– didn't dull the ache deep down inside. That was something she was just going to have to live with.

Both Terje and his father were already seated at the table when she went downstairs at seven-thirty the next morning. Leif was dressed for business, while Terje was wearing T-shirt and jeans, reminding her only too forcibly of their first meeting.

'I hope you found your bed comfortable,' said the older man solicitously.

'Very, thank you,' Kirsten assured him.

Sliding into her seat, she made herself look directly at Terje, offering a steady, 'Good morning,' and receiving an equable reply. Last night's incident had been relegated to its proper place, it seemed; not important enough to generate any lingering ill-will. She wished she could put the memory aside as easily.

'I imagine Rune needs a lot of sleep at his age,' she remarked for want of anything else to say, helping herself to bread and cheese. 'Especially after being up so late.'

'He doesn't like to feel he might be missing anything,' returned Leif on a humorous note. He added to Terje, 'What time do you plan to be back?'

'Late,' returned his son. 'I decided we'd go to Trondheim today instead of Sunday. We can fly out over Hardanger before heading north. You see far more of the fjords from the air.'

'A good idea,' Leif agreed. 'Then you have the whole weekend free. You will enjoy Trondheim, Kirsten. It was the capital city of Norway in medieval times.'

Still adjusting to the sudden change of plan, she said diffidently, 'Will I need any warm clothing?'

He shook his head. 'Most people imagine it a cold place because of its position, but the summers are warm. Of course, winter is the best time of all to go there. Most of our skiing and skating champions are from the Trondheim area. You should visit us later in the year when the snows come.'

Kirsten murmured some appropriate reply, not caring this time to look at Terje. Leif might be prepared to extend his goodwill towards future relations, but neither his son nor his father would be in agreement.

She donned jeans and shirt herself for the journey, and took along a sweater. It was a bare ten-minute drive to the sheltered little bay where Terje kept his float plane. A four-seater Cessna painted white with black lettering picked out boldly against the fuselage, it was already fuelled and waiting.

Kirsten shrank from touching any controls as she buckled herself into the front passenger seat, wondering what she would do if something happened to Terje while they were up there. It was unlikely that he was suddenly going to keel over, she reassured herself. There was no question about his fitness.

She watched him go through the pre-flight checks and bring the engine to life, comforted by his attention to detail. With the weather still holding, the water surface looked calm enough, but her nerves tensed again as he taxied the plane out into the open water and she felt waves slapping at the floats.

There was a roar as he opened the throttle, sending them skimming forward in a cloud of feathery spray. She felt the machine rise and trim forward on the floats, then they were clear and climbing, coming round in a wide turn to head south.

Spread below, the landscape was magnificent: a multitude of islands and waterways, of pine-clad hills and mountain peaks. Kirsten was entranced, devouring the scene with nose pressed against the side-window, nervousness forgotten. This was the Norway of her imagination—wild and beautiful; a land barely touched by modern civilisation.

Hardangerfjord was a kaleidoscope of colour, its blue waters bounded by lofty, snow-capped mountains striped with countless waterfalls, and riven by valleys carpeted in brilliant emerald-green. Terje flew right up and over the

Hardangerjokelen glacier with its spilling, sun-sparkled ice flow before finally turning north.

'You have very little to say for yourself this morning,' he commented as Kirsten settled back into her seat.

'I've been too busy just looking,' she conceded. 'With all this to go at, I'm surprised you want to spend any time at all in England. I know we have some lovely areas, but nothing like this!'

'It's good to have a change of scene at times too,' he returned. 'You have more contrast in England, if rather less challenge.'

'Do you spend all your spare time tramping the country-side?' she asked.

'A great deal of it in summer, yes.'

'Always alone?'

'Not necessarily. Sometimes with a group.'

'All men, of course!'

He smiled briefly. 'We have no objection to women joining in providing they're capable of keeping up.'

She kept the question casual. 'Does Inger like to hike?'

'On occasion.' He cast another glance. 'Why?'

'She just doesn't look the type.'

'Looks,' he said, 'can be deceptive. Inger enjoys all manner of pastimes. Bergen has its share of nightclubs and discotheques, along with everything else.'

'But you're not too keen on that form of pastime yourself?'

The shrug was light. 'Given the choice, I'd rather be outdoors than in, but I'm not averse to organised entertainment.'

She would almost prefer a renewal of hostilities to this kind of banal exchange, Kirsten reflected wryly, lapsing into silence again. Here, in the close confines of the cabin, she found his masculine presence overpowering. There was something sensual in the very way he handled the controls; an air of command that tremored her senses. He would be a dominant lover too—in charge all the time.

She stole a glance at him, feeling the muscles about her heart contract as her eyes came to rest on the firmly moulded mouth. His physical attraction was only a part of it; she was already coming dangerously close to allowing her deeper emotions to become involved. Terje might have his faults, but his basic integrity was in no doubt. Jean must have been mad to give him up for someone as shallow as Nils Torvund.

Unless, of course, she hadn't anticipated being found out. If it had depended on Nils's discretion, though, Kirsten doubted if he would have stayed silent even if Terje hadn't actually caught them in the act. The way he had been so quick to point out her own resemblance to the other girl indicated a certain malicious intent. There was a whole lot of jealousy there, if she weren't mistaken.

'Is Georg with Brulands?' she asked.

The reply was slow in coming, as if the question itself had taken him by surprise. 'No, he's in the retail business. Nils is general manager.'

That might explain the jealousy, Kirsten reflected. Perhaps Nils had expected to join the Bruland hierarchy when his father married into the family. It would certainly have been a step up.

Terje made no attempt to keep the conversational ball rolling. He seemed to have retreated again, face austere. Kirsten closed heart and mind to everything but the untamed beauty of the scenery, filing away the detail in order to present a word picture to her father when she got back home. Whether he would ever get to see it for himself was open to doubt. Only if he were specifically invited might he even consider paying his cousins a visit, and that seemed unlikely on the face of it.

Built on a peninsula between river and fjord, and laced with canals, Trondheim was a cross between Amsterdam and Venice in a wooden kind of way. Rows of warehouses, each painted a different colour, stood on stilts along the riverside. The fjord waterfront teemed with fishing boats and pleasure craft of every size and shape, along with the coastal steamers which plied north from here to the Lofoten Islands in the 'Land of the Midnight Sun'.

Kirsten found the town itself surprisingly spacious. As in Bergen, and most other Norwegian towns which had relied so heavily on wood for building, there had been devastating fires from time to time, and broad avenues had replaced many of the narrow twisting streets of medieval days, but, as Leif had intimated, the ambience was still there–especially in the vast wooden baroque palace that was the northern residence of the royal family.

Although she was hardly expecting to see the original home of the Bruland family, it was still a bitter disappointment to discover that the site itself was now covered by a modern apartment block.

'You might have told me,' she said accusingly to Terje.

'Does that mean you wouldn't have wanted to come to Trondheim at all if I had?' he asked.

'Well. . .no,' she admitted. She added quickly, 'I really am grateful to you for taking the time to bring me. I had the idea of tracing my roots right back to source, that's all.'

His shrug was dismissive. 'I'd say you were close enough. If you've seen all you want to see for now, we'd better get some lunch. It's almost one-thirty.'

'I hadn't realised,' she apologised, aware that he would

normally have eaten closer to midday. 'You should have said something.'

'I just did,' he returned on a dry note. 'If you've no objection to seafood, there's a restaurant just across the road there.'

Accustomed to skipping lunch more often than not back home, Kirsten realised suddenly that she was hungry herself. 'No objection at all,' she assured him.

The restaurant was almost empty at this hour, the service quick and efficient. Unable to read the menu, and reluctant to keep asking what each item was, Kirsten left it to Terje to order for them both, and thoroughly enjoyed the poached trout and sour cream.

'How long is it since you were last in Trondheim?' she asked over coffee.

'This last winter,' he said. 'I came up to ski at Oppdal. The Dovrefjell further south has snow all year round. I usually manage a weekend or two during the summer.'

She would be back in harness at the surgery then, with all this just a far-away dream. She would miss it, Kirsten acknowledged. The whole way of life here appealed to her. Not that there was anything to stop her from indulging in more outdoor activities back home, of course, but no woman with any sense at all went hiking the countryside on her own, and who did she know who might share the enthusiasm?

'Now that Sunday is going to be free, is the offer to take me sailing still open?' she asked on a diffident note.

'If you want to go.'

From the way he said it, it sounded as if it didn't matter either way to him, she judged. And why should it? He was only spending time with her at all because his father had made it plain that he expected some effort to be made. Whether he had actually planned last night's little scene she couldn't be sure, but there was no doubt in her mind that if she had proved willing he would have gone all the way. The easy and purely physical passion of any man for any woman, that was all it had been.

'It isn't important,' she said.

Terje made no attempt to offer assurances. He seemed in no hurry to move, although the tables were now being reset for *middag*. With night still far away, Kirsten supposed there was plenty of time to make the return flight, but she didn't feel like doing any more sightseeing in the company of a man who only too obviously would prefer to be somewhere else. Why prolong the day any further than necessary?

'I'm ready to go back whenever you are,' she said. 'Don't feel you have to stay out the whole day for me.'

He observed her dispassionately. 'Bored already?'

'Not at all,' she denied. 'But you must be.'

'If and when I am, I'll let you know. I thought we might go to Hell before we leave.' He smiled faintly at her expression. 'A short journey by train in this case. How do you like the idea of sending your parents a card postmarked from Hell?'

'They don't know I'm here,' she returned.

'Then don't you think it's time you let them know?'

Kirsten looked him in the eye, holding the cynical regard with an effort. 'Why bother? Your father is the only one with any interest in renewing our relationship, and even he isn't all that enthusiastic about it. Perhaps it would be better just to leave things the way they always were.'

'You can't do that,' he said flatly. 'Not unless you're prepared to tell a whole pack of lies about where you've been and what you've been doing. I doubt very much whether 'Far would allow it anyway.'

'Even if it means upsetting your grandfather still further?'

'Rune doesn't have to be involved.'

'Providing we made no more personal visits.' Her voice was taut. 'I'd rather Dad knew nothing about it than tell him he isn't allowed to come here!'

'That isn't what I'm saying,' came the unmoved reply. 'Only that it would be better if Rune knew nothing of it.'

'There's an alternative,' she said carefully. 'You or your father–or even both of you–could come to England.'

His glance dropped to the coffee-cup she had been holding between her hands for the last five minutes. 'That will be cold by now. Would you like some more?'

Kirsten shook her head, ruefully aware of having made an offer that he for one was hardly going to find irresistible. 'No, thanks.'

'Then we'll go,' he said.

Hell was a bare half-hour away. It boasted a neat little station, a scatter of pretty wooden houses and a church set among birch trees. There was also a general store, and a tiny post office, to which all the passengers just alighted from the train duly flocked.

'They think I'm in France,' Kirsten protested when Terje repeated his suggestion that she send her parents a postcard. 'I can't just drop it on them out of the blue!'

'It will take a few days to reach them,' he pointed out. 'You can telephone home before that and tell them the truth.'

'The truth being that I made the mistake of thinking I could wipe out sixty years of prejudice.' She made no effort to keep the bitterness from her voice. 'I should never have come!'

'You don't wipe out sixty years overnight,' he returned hardily.

'It wouldn't be wiped out at all if it were left up to you!' she accused, giving way to the anger flooding through her. 'You're not just prejudiced against my family, it's me personally, isn't it? You won't give me a chance!'

They were drawing curious glances from those both entering and leaving the little post office. Kirsten moved abruptly to start walking in the direction of the station, heedless to whether Terje followed her or not. She felt so churned up inside–wanting him and hating him at one and the same time. There was no give in him at all.

He caught up with her before she had gone more than a few yards, falling into step at her side. When he spoke it was with an inflexion quite different from that of a few moments ago.

'Perhaps we should start again.'

Totally thrown, Kirsten hardly knew what to answer. If the offer was genuine then she was more than ready to agree, but the change in attitude was so sudden.

'Why now?' she got out.

Terje took her by the arm, drawing her to a halt. His fingers were light in their grasp, yet burned like fire through the sleeves of her shirt. Devoid for once of cynicism, the blue eyes held an expression that made her heart turn over.

'Because it's time I stopped blaming you for reminding me of something I thought I'd put aside,' he said. 'You might look like Jean, you might even act like her at times, but there are differences. I've simply been closing my eyes to them.'

The sun was behind him, highlighting the gold of his hair. This close, her neck ached from looking up at him. She wanted desperately to be closer still, to have his arms about her, his lips on hers.

'I'd like to,' she murmured. 'Start again, I mean.'

His smile was slow, his gaze dropping to her mouth as if in recognition of her thoughts. 'We still have a week.'

Beyond which she wasn't going to look, Kirsten determined, feeling suddenly revitalised. A lot could happen in a week.

'I think I will send that card,' she said. 'And I'll make the call this weekend.' She hesitated, searching his face, still not wholly certain. 'Will you be prepared to speak with my father?'

'Better, I think, that he speak with *my* father initially, but I've no objection. Just as long as you don't expect Rune to change his views.'

Having this member of the family change his was enough for the present, she thought as he turned her back towards the post office.

It was coming up to five-thirty by the time they got back to Trondheim. Not hungry herself, but anticipating that Terje would want to eat again before undertaking the journey back to Bergen, Kirsten was surprised when he called a taxi to take them direct from the train to the seaplane harbour. It would be gone nine when they landed, she reckoned.

After eating lunch so late, he could last out until they reached home, he said when she mentioned the matter.

She waited on the quayside while he went to settle the bill for landing fees and refuelling charges. Although still high in the sky, the sun had lost a lot of its warmth, making her glad to don the sweater she had carried around all day. Even more now she was glad that they had come to Trondheim. Terje seemed ready at last to make a real effort towards achieving an understanding. He was going to be tied up with business matters for the greater part of the coming week, of course, but the whole weekend still lay ahead.

Except that she was supposed to be spending tomorrow

with Nils, she recalled with a sudden drop in spirits. It was the very last thing she felt like doing, but how did she get out of it now?

Terje looked rather pensive himself, she thought as she watched him approach.

'Something wrong?' she asked as soon as he was in earshot.

'Nothing disastrous,' he answered levelly. 'But I'm afraid we're going to be stuck here for the night.'

CHAPTER SIX

'WHY?' Kirsten said blankly.

'Fuel leak,' came the reply. 'We seemed to have used more than normal on the way here, so I asked for a check to be made. They can't get hold of the part needed until tomorrow.'

'I see.' Kirsten tried to bring her mind to bear on the ramifications of this new development. 'I suppose the first thing is to let your father know.'

'I already did,' Terje acknowledged, adding evenly, 'I also asked him to telephone Nils and tell him you wouldn't be able to see him tomorrow after all.'

For a wild moment she wondered if this was a deliberate ploy to keep her from doing just that, but there was no hint of ulterior motivation in the blue eyes.

'So what do we do now?' she asked.

'The only thing we can do,' he said. 'We find a hotel for the night.'

'But we don't have anything with us.'

'I doubt if a lack of luggage will bar us,' Terje returned drily. 'Although we can always go and buy whatever you consider essential. It need not be one of the large hotels. Even the smaller ones have all the usual facilities. There's one near the harbour that I've used before.'

There was no other choice, Kirsten was bound to concede. If the part didn't turn up tomorrow, they might even be stuck here all weekend. Apart from the lack of overnight gear, the idea wasn't off-putting. The more time they spent together the better–so far as she was concerned, at any rate.

Terje called up another taxi to take them to the hotel. At this hour, the front lobby was busy with people both coming and going, some dressed for the evening, some still wearing the same kind of casual clothing they had on themselves. Terje spoke to the receptionist in Norwegian, so Kirsten couldn't be sure what explanation he gave, but their lack of luggage appeared to cause no great concern.

Trondheim obviously didn't get as busy in summer as Bergen, for rooms were readily available. There was an in-house restaurant, Terje advised as they moved away from the desk, also a small shop where they could purchase any necessary toilet items.

Small it certainly was, but at least they were able to get toothbrushes and paste. Kirsten had hated to think of facing the morning without being able to clean her teeth. With a comb and lipstick already in her tote bag, she could manage, although it meant wearing the same clothes again, of course.

The rooms were adjoining each other on the third floor. As in all Norwegian hotels, they were scrupulously clean and comfortable. Kirsten vaguely noted the communicating door in passing, but was more interested in the *en-suite* bathroom. A shower was what she craved most at the moment.

By seven o'clock, when Terje knocked on the door, she was as ready as she could be in the circumstances. Fortunately, her blue chambray shirt had stayed reasonably crisp and fresh over the day. Never having worn a lot of make-up, she felt no particular self-consciousness over her lipstick-only appearance, and was unprepared for the sudden teasing light in Terje's eyes as he viewed her.

'You look like a well-scrubbed schoolgirl,' he said.

Providing he didn't treat her like a schoolgirl, came the fleeting thought.

'Needs must,' she rejoined lightly. 'You'll just have to turn a blind eye.'

'Did I say that I didn't like it?' The teasing note was still there, but with a subtle difference. 'You have little need of enhancements.'

Caught and held by the blue gaze, Kirsten felt her heart do a double flip. She wanted to laugh out loud in sudden exhilaration.

'I never thought I'd hear myself say this,' she admitted, 'but I'm starving hungry! Will we be allowed in the restaurant?'

'Of course,' he said. 'There's no dress code here.'

That was possibly true, but none of the other diners looked quite as casual. Kirsten felt the censure of all eyes as they made their way to a table, and was glad to sit down and tuck her jean-clad legs out of sight.

Reluctant again to ask Terje to translate the menu, she took a chance and ordered *fiskeboller*, which turned out, as she had anticipated, to be fishballs. Served poached and laid in a bechamel sauce, they were delicious. Terje chose fish too, deep-fried fillets of flounder and french fries, with a cucumber salad on the side—most of which Kirsten ate.

She shook her head when he asked if she would like dessert.

'Not if you want the plane to take off tomorrow!' she smiled, then sobered to add, 'Is there likely to be any difficulty getting the part?'

'There shouldn't be.' He looked at her reflectively. 'Would it worry you if we were delayed longer?'

'Only in the sense that I can't visualise spending the whole weekend in the same clothes,' she acknowledged, and he gave a laugh.

'Feminine priorities! There are shops in Trondheim.'

And she had her credit card with her, Kirsten reminded herself. Even if she had felt nothing for Terje before, she would have found this new and relaxed version irresistible, she knew.

As Trondheim was so much further north, the sun didn't set until eleven-thirty, and the light never really faded from the sky at all. The two of them strolled about the harbour until gone midnight, the atmosphere between them one of ease, yet with an underlying anticipation of events still to come. Kirsten was only too well aware of what was probably going to happen, and didn't care. It was beyond her to deny the emotions Terje aroused. She wanted him with every fibre of her being.

The hotel lobby was quiet when they returned, the desk unmanned for the moment. Going up in the lift, she could hear her own heartbeats, and wondered if Terje could hear them too. Stealing a glance at the carved profile, she began to wonder whether she had perhaps misread his intent, then he turned his head and met her eyes and she knew she hadn't. She felt herself drowning in the deep blue sea of his gaze, her limbs turning to water.

'This time,' he said softly, and she knew at once what he meant. This time there would be no backing away by either party.

They reached her bedroom door first. Her fingers trembled as she tried to fit the key in the lock. Terje took it from her and turned it around, sliding it in smoothly and ushering her ahead of him through the opened doorway with a hand at the centre of her back.

Despite the drawn curtains, the room wasn't wholly in darkness. Terje made no attempt to switch on a light, closing the door gently and sliding the internal lock with an audible click. They were safe now from intrusion, came the reassuring thought as he turned her into his arms. Safe until they themselves chose to end their confinement.

His mouth felt so different this time, almost delicate in its seeking. Kirsten answered with honesty, feeling the delicious languor stealing into her limbs, the uncurling warmth deep in the pit of her stomach. She had hoped it would be like this, lips brushing, nibbling, stimulating her senses with finesse. His jaw felt smooth against hers. She breathed in his evocative male scent, filling her head with his essence.

This time there was no harshness in the invasion of his tongue, just a devastating sensuality that induced a like response. The warmth became heat, spiralling from a central core, drawing her deeper and deeper into its vortex. The blood throbbed in her veins, sang in her ears, pulsated her heart. Her whole body was on fire with it.

The buttons of her shirt gave easily to his touch. Light and low-cut, her bra proved no barrier either. She drew in a shuddering breath as the long lean fingers slid beneath the flimsy material to explore the shape of her, gentle yet not so gentle, teasing her nipple to a throbbing peak. He was in total command, and they both knew it, but she had no objection. She wanted to be taken–to belong wholly and completely to this man.

As before, he slid an arm beneath her to lift and carry her across to the bed, laying her down on the cover to stand over her for a brief moment of pure contemplative power before reaching to unfasten the remaining buttons and slide the shirt-sleeves down her arms. The clip of her bra was at the front, which fazed him not at all. Kirsten thrilled to the look in the blue eyes as he surveyed her nudity.

High and firm, her breasts rested in his cupped palms as if made to measure. She quivered as he bent his head to run the very tip of his tongue round first one aureola and then the other, gasping as his teeth closed on her nipple. The sensation was exquisite; she felt her insides turn fluid, her limbs go weak. She ran frantic fingers into the thickness of his hair, torn between an urge to push him away and a need to hold him even closer; unable to bear it yet reluctant to have it stop.

'Terje!' she pleaded, and wasn't sure what it was she was asking. 'Terje!'

'*Jeg her,*' he said.

The timbre of his voice, low and vibrant, made her tremble. Everything about him made her tremble—not in fear but in sheer anticipation of what was still to come. Reaching down, he removed her shoes one by one and dropped them to the floor at the side of the bed, then came back to unfasten the waistband of her jeans and slide the material over her hips. The room was heated against the night chill so there was no sensation of coldness when he peeled the jeans away from her legs, but she shivered just the same.

She was wearing nothing but a pair of scanty nylon briefs beneath. Terje made no immediate move to remove those too. Instead, he splayed his fingers lightly across her bare stomach, moving them in a caress that was soothing and stimulating at one and the same time. Bending, he put his lips to a point just below and behind her ear, tracing the outline of her face down to the point of her jaw, then on down the length of her throat to seek the vulnerable hollow with its fluttering pulse.

Kirsten closed her eyes, feeling the slow downward drift of his hand and hearing the mounting thunder in her ears. The first gentle brush of his thumb against the narrow band of her briefs brought her heart into her throat. Her thigh muscles went into sudden spasm as the tip of a finger slid into the silky cluster, clenching involuntarily against the threatened intrusion.

He lifted his head to find her mouth again, cherishing her lips until she relaxed and responded. This time there was no resistance, just a deep indrawn breath as his hand slid between her thighs to seek the moist heat of her womanhood. A moan broke from her lips as he deepened the caress with a slow sensuality that reached every nerve-ending in her body. He was inside her, possessing her, driving her wild with the exquisite torment, until a shuddering white-hot pleasure flooded body and mind together.

Floating, she was dimly aware of his movements, but it wasn't until he lowered himself to her again that she realised he had removed his own clothing. His skin felt slightly damp, the muscle hard beneath. She ran light fingers over one broad shoulder and down the length of his arm, intoxicated by the feel of him, the strength of him. The complete male: dominant, masterful, wholly exciting.

Taking her hand, he guided her to him, groaning low in his throat at her first tentative caress. She grew bolder as realisation of *her* power took hold, watching his face with a sense of elation that she could give him as intense pleasure as he had given her. Desire grew in her. She needed to be closer, to have him inside her, an integral part of her— to be utterly possessed by him.

When he came down over her at last she was avid in her readiness. He entered her smoothly and commandingly, inciting a response over which she had no control. She lost all sense of time and place and was conscious only of the driving force of his loins, the rising clamour of her heartbeats and the final pulsing implosion.

It was broad daylight when she opened her eyes, and for a moment she couldn't think where she was. Only when she moved, and felt the deep-down ache in her body, did memory return.

She was alone, although the sound of rushing water from the bathroom told its own story. She had spent the night in Terje's arms, held close of necessity by the confines of the single bed. Her sleep had been deep, for she hadn't felt him go.

Kirsten closed her eyes again, the better to recall the sheer ecstasy of their lovemaking. She had given herself to him with total abandonment—held absolutely nothing back. He knew her now more intimately than Nick had ever known her. It was difficult to believe that a mere few days ago she hadn't even been aware of Terje's existence. From that very first moment she had set eyes on him, she had been inexorably drawn.

Was it possible to fall in love in a few days? she wondered, and decided it had to be, because she had done it. Terje was everything Nick wasn't—a man she could both trust and respect. Nick had hurt her pride more than her heart, if she were honest about it. She hadn't been enough for him. If last night had taught her anything, it was to stop blaming herself for that failure. It was the singer who made the song, and Terje was a virtuoso.

An expert lover, perhaps, came the sudden and sobering thought, but what else did he feel for her? She had made herself available, and he had taken advantage of the offer, but it didn't have to mean anything more than that. The very fact that he had left her without attempting to waken her this morning might even suggest that desire itself had ebbed.

The shower had stopped, she realised, although how long ago she couldn't be sure. Sitting up, she saw her clothing lying neatly folded on the other bed, too far away to reach for. With the bathroom door likely to open any minute, she stayed put. It was one thing to have Terje see her nude in the throes of lovemaking, quite another to have him catch her standing there in full daylight without a stitch. His own clothes were gone, so she could only assume that he had them with him.

Her heart jerked as the door came open. He was fully dressed, his hair towel-dried and finger-combed from the look of it. He paused there in the doorway when he saw she was awake, looking across at her with a slow smile pulling at his lips.

'I couldn't get through to my room without going outside, so I used your shower,' he said. 'There's another dry towel.'

'No problem.' Kirsten was surprised by the steadiness of her voice. 'What time is it?'

'Seven-thirty. No hurry. Even if they have the part, the plane is unlikely to be ready until this afternoon.'

'No, of course not.' She cast around for something else to say, lacking the courage simply to stretch out an inviting hand. 'When will you know?'

'I'll telephone after we have breakfast.'

He studied her for a moment, as if trying to read something in her face, then he came over to the bed, sitting down on the mattress-edge to draw her up to him in an embrace that set her pulses clamouring. The kiss was passionate but controlled, leaving her somewhere between heaven and earth. She gazed at him dazedly when he drew away again, trying not to let her emotions run away with her. Whatever else he might or might not feel, the desire obviously still lived.

He touched her jaw where the skin was reddened, then ran a hand over the golden stubble lining his own jawline. 'I need a shave. Give me a knock when you're ready.'

Kirsten watched him cross to the outer door. She felt all churned up inside, hardly knowing what to think. 'We still have a week,' he had said yesterday afternoon, but for what exactly? Her chance resemblance to the girl who had let him down so badly had to be a stumbling-block on the way to any deeper relationship, even if he wanted it.

But perhaps not an insurmountable one, she thought on a surge of determination. It was up to her to show him just how different she really was from Jean–to teach him to trust her. Time was going to be the problem. She would need to use every minute of it.

He was ready and waiting when she knocked on his door some half an hour later. The blue eyes held a curious expression as she reached up to kiss him warmly on the mouth.

'An eye for an eye,' she said softly, and he laughed, drawing her into the room and closing the door against any passers-by before taking her in his arms.

Shorn of the morning stubble, his jaw was smooth against her skin, the subtle tang of aftershave a stimulant in itself, the feel of his hand at her breast even more so. If he had suggested going back to bed there and then, she would have gone without protest. It was a disappointment when he put her firmly away from him.

'Breakfast,' he said, 'and then the telephone. After which we'll know how much time we have to spare.'

Another day wouldn't go amiss, Kirsten reflected, but she refrained from voicing the thought. She needed to tread carefully. Going overboard too soon could ruin everything.

The restaurant was busy. It took them almost an hour to have breakfast. Seated across from Terje, with conversation between them the most amicable it had ever been, Kirsten allowed herself a cautious optimism. Learning to be at ease with one another was half the battle. Man couldn't live on love alone–or woman either, for that matter. She knew already that she could happily spend the rest of her life with this one, even if it meant leaving everything familiar. Home was where the heart was, and hers was right here.

Terje left her sitting in the lobby while he went to telephone about the plane.

'It will be ready after lunch,' he said on return. 'We'll be home in time for *middag*.' The pause was brief, his expression neutral. 'I rang to tell Far. He said Nils was very disappointed, and wants to spend Sunday with you instead.'

'But I don't want to spend it with him,' Kirsten responded. 'I've no interest in Nils.'

'You accepted his invitation.'

'Only because he made it difficult to say no.' She tried not to sound too anxious to convince him. 'Anyway, you said you'd take me sailing.'

He said levelly, 'Last night doesn't tie you to anything.'

It didn't tie him to anything either, she took him to mean, and felt her spirits take a swift and heart-renching dive. Pride came to her rescue, lifting her chin and lending a certain insouciance to her voice.

'I'm fully aware of that. We're two people who just happened to go to bed together.'

'Not just happened,' came the response. 'We both of us knew it was coming. All I'm saying is—'

'Not to take it too seriously,' she finished for him. She forced herself to meet and hold his gaze. 'I'm not a schoolgirl, Terje.'

The blue eyes were veiled. 'No,' he agreed, 'you are not. What would you like to do this morning?'

Asked that same question only a few minutes ago, Kirsten would have known exactly what she wanted to do. Right now, she was too disconsolate to care. Her own fault for allowing her emotions to run away with her, she acknowledged hollowly. Terje felt nothing for her beyond a purely physical desire; he had made that clear enough.

'Whatever you think best,' she said. 'You know the place.'

'Then you might like to see the Folk Museum,' he suggested. 'And the cathedral is worth more than the passing glance we gave it yesterday. There could be a market too.'

'Sounds good,' she agreed, trying to instil some enthusiasm into her voice. 'Enough to take us through till lunch, anyway.'

More than enough, as it turned out, and worthwhile too, despite her depressed interest in sightseeing. Terje settled for a couple of hamburgers and a coffee from a fast-food outlet for lunch. Not in the least bit hungry herself, Kirsten picked at a chicken roll and drank a Coke, while attempting to keep up a bright and breezy conversation. Terje's responses came readily enough, lending strength to the notion that her apparent lack of emotional involvement concerning last night's events was a relief to him. As she had said herself, they were simply two people who had spent the night together. It happened all the time.

They found the plane ready and waiting. Terje left her to strap herself into her seat while he went to settle his account. Once in the air, he flew a full circuit over Trondheim to give her the benefit of an overall view before heading south. Kirsten was able to see for the first time how the Nid river made an abrupt loop before pouring its waters into the fjord, forming the triangular peninsula on which the city was built. Erosion from both sides of the narrow strip still connecting it to the mainland might eventually make it a true island kingdom.

Whether that happened or not, this was likely to be the last glimpse she ever had, Kirsten reflected. In fact, the way she felt at present, this was likely to be her one and only visit to Norway at all. With a full five days–and six more nights–still to go before she boarded ship for home, she was going to find it difficult to keep up this act of hers, but she would give it her best shot, she vowed. Anything was better than having Terje guess how far and fast she had fallen.

The flight back was uneventful so far as untoward happenings went, although the scenery was an event in itself. She could love this land, Kirsten thought as they circled in over the Byfjorden. It had beauty, culture, a fascinating history and a lifestyle that appealed to her greatly. Diluted though it might be, the blood still ran in her veins.

Terje had seemed preoccupied during the flight. Driving back to the house, he had little to say, although his manner didn't seem constrained. A lack of anything worth saying, Kirsten gathered, silent herself. She felt weary and stiff from sitting still for so long, and eager for a shower and change of clothing. Later, she would contact Nils and tell him she would be glad to spend Sunday with him, even if it was a downright lie. That would let Terje off the hook.

Leif greeted the pair of them as casually as if they had just been out for a stroll. Enforced stop-overs weren't all that rare when it came to small plane flying, Kirsten supposed. The weather alone could provide enough reason. It had been raining when they landed, and although it had stopped now the sky was dull and overcast with a threat of more to come. Hopefully, it would clear again for the Midsummer Eve celebrations on Monday.

With her hair shampooed and brush-dried, and her face lightly made-up, she put on a lemon cotton shift and stepped into low-heeled sandals. The smile she tried on herself through the mirror looked totally false; she made an effort to lighten it. Yearning for the unattainable was a total waste of time. Last night had to be put aside.

Except that it was impossible to do that with Terje

around. Wearing pale grey trousers and darker-toned shirt, he made her pulses leap the moment she set eyes on him.

'You were going to telephone your parents,' he reminded her at dinner. 'Are they likely to be in on a Saturday evening?'

'I imagine so,' Kirsten acknowledged. 'They don't like going out a great deal.'

'There is nothing wrong in preferring to stay home,' put in Leif mildly, as if recognising a certain defensiveness in her tone. 'I often do myself these days. I'm pleased that you decided to tell them where you are. Perhaps I might speak with your father myself after you finish?'

'I'm sure he'll be delighted to hear from you,' she said. 'Once he's over the initial shock.'

'You also have to contact Nils,' he added. 'He was very insistent.'

Kirsten waited a brief and hopeful moment for Terje to say something before answering, but he made no comment. 'I'll do that first,' she confirmed with reluctance, still not wholly certain what she was going to tell the other man. She didn't want to spend Sunday with him, but neither did she want Terje to feel obligated to entertain her any further than he already had.

Rune was being his usual taciturn self, ignoring her totally. He looked somehow more shrunken tonight, Kirsten thought, his skin almost translucent. At eighty-four, his remaining years had to be limited; he must recognise that fact himself. It made it even more vital that she should reach him, although how she had no idea. Terje had refused to negotiate an amnesty, which left only Leif. It was worth a try.

It was Leif who supplied the number for her to ring Nils. More than half anticipating that he would be out somewhere at this hour on a Saturday evening, she was thrown to hear his voice.

'I have been waiting for you to call,' he said, sounding somewhat aggrieved. 'When did you get back?'

'A couple of hours ago,' she was bound to confess. 'I'm sorry, Nils. I should have phoned right away.' She paused, searching for the right words. 'About tomorrow, I—'

'I'll call for you at nine,' he said, and rang off before she could offer any objection.

Which left her with very little choice, Kirsten conceded wryly, like it or not. She had to force herself to lift the receiver again for the call to England, wishing suddenly that she could cancel out the whole of the past few days. If she hadn't made this trip in the first place, she would never have known Terje.

Hearing her father's voice on the line brought a wave of homesickness. 'Hello, Dad,' she said.

'Kirsten!' From his tone, relief was the uppermost emotion. 'We were getting worried because we hadn't heard from you. Is everything all right?'

'Everything is fine,' she assured him, trying to infuse enthusiasm into her voice. 'I'm not in France, though.'

'You're not?' He sounded taken aback. 'But I thought—'

'You thought what I wanted you to think,' she interrupted gently. 'Because I didn't want you to know what I was really planning until I'd tested the water.' She took a deep breath. 'I'm in Norway. Bergen, to be exact. Staying at the home of your cousin, Leif Bruland. He wants to speak to you himself when I've finished.'

The silence was prolonged. Kirsten was beginning to think the line had gone dead when her father finally spoke again.

'I can hardly believe it! After all this time! How did you know where to find him?'

'Through Brulands, of course.'

'You mean you simply went there and demanded to see him?'

Kirsten had to laugh. 'More or less. Anyway, it wasn't nearly as bad as it sounds. He not only saw me, but insisted that I come back here to the house to stay. He didn't even know about your attempt to renew relations. It was his father, Rune, who made that decision. He doesn't speak any English, which makes things a bit difficult, but both Leif and Terje are fluent.'

'Who is Terje?' John Harley sounded bemused.

'Leif's son. He's a managing director. He flew me up to Trondheim to see where Grandmother was born. There's another branch of the family in Oslo, but I shan't have time to meet them. I'm booked on Friday's ferry back to Newcastle, so I'll be home some time Saturday evening.' She was talking too much and too fast, Kirsten knew; she took a hold on herself. 'I can tell you everything in detail when I see you. I'd better put Leif on now.'

The latter came and took the receiver from her when she called him through to the room from where she was making the call. '*Hello*, *kusine*,' he said, then switched to English to add warmly, 'So your daughter has brought us together at last.'

Kirsten looked blindly out of the window, only half listening to the one-sided conversation. The one with whom she most wanted to be was Terje, only it obviously wasn't to be. He had taken what was offered, the way any man would—might even be prepared to do the same again if the opportunity arose, but that was as far as it went for him. Allowing herself to fall in love with him had been foolish in the extreme, considering what she knew. He mistrusted English women *en masse*, that was what it boiled down to.

'Your mother wishes to speak to you,' said Leif, holding out the receiver to her.

Kirsten took the instrument from him, lightening her voice. 'Hello, Mum!'

'You've given us quite a shock,' came the response on a note of faint reproof. 'You should have told us what you were planning to do.'

'You'd neither of you have approved,' Kirsten defended, still sticking to the light note. 'This way, you needn't have known anything about it if I'd failed to make contact.' Leif had gone back to the living-room, leaving her free to add, 'What do you think to our Norwegian cousin?'

'He sounds very nice,' her mother acknowledged. There was a pause, a slight change of tone. 'Darling, are you all right? You don't sound yourself at all.'

Trust a mother's ear to pick up the nuances, Kirsten reflected wryly. 'I'm absolutely fine,' she assured her. 'Couldn't be better! Norway is a beautiful country, you and Dad must come and see it yourselves some time.'

'Leif already invited us to visit, but I don't know whether we will. Your father is happy just to know that things have been sorted out at last. Anyway, I think we'd better ring off. This call must be costing a lot of money. We'll see you next weekend.'

The way she felt at the moment, she wished she were taking the boat tomorrow instead of Friday, Kirsten thought as she replaced the receiver. There was a sailing this evening, arriving at Newcastle on Monday. She might still be able to get on it.

And what explanation would she give Leif for such a sudden change of plan? came the following thought. A plea of homesickness was hardly going to sound convincing. She had to see it through. There was no other way.

CHAPTER SEVEN

RUNE WAS watching television when Kirsten went back to the living-room, while Leif was reading a magazine. Terje was missing.

'I'm very grateful for the way you've reacted to all this, Leif,' she said impulsively. 'I did rather drop on you.'

'Someone had to make the first move if we were ever to settle the matter,' he returned. 'I look forward to meeting your parents before too long. Do you think they might come to Norway themselves?'

'I'm not sure. They're not great travellers.' She hesitated before tagging on diffidently, 'Is there any chance of you coming to England some time?'

'It's possible.' He obviously wasn't about to tie himself down to any promises. 'Terje went down to the lake to take a look at the boat. Tomorrow should be a good day for sailing.'

Kirsten accepted the change of subject, wryly aware that there were limitations even to Leif's interest in furthering the relationship. 'Will you be going out with him?' she asked on what she hoped was a casual note.

He shook his head. 'I have other arrangements. Did you speak to Nils?'

'He's picking me up at nine,' she confirmed, and registered a fleeting change of expression in the blue eyes so like his son's. She added swiftly, 'I hope that's all right? I'd hate it to seem as if I'm using your home like a hotel.'

'Of course you are not,' he assured her. 'You must come and go as you like while you are here.' His regard was steady. 'Nils is very much a ladies' man.'

She returned his gaze, wondering just how much Terje had told him. Not the whole story, or Nils surely wouldn't still be welcome here in his home. 'Is that a warning?' she asked lightly.

Leif gave a brief smile. 'A word of advice, perhaps. Sometimes the heart can rule the head.'

Didn't she know it? came the rueful thought. She said firmly, 'I'm not drawn to Nils that way, so mine isn't at risk, but I appreciate the concern.' Pretending to smother a yawn, she added, 'I know it's only half-past nine, but would you mind if I went to bed? I didn't get much sleep last night.'

The moment she'd said it she could feel her colour coming up, but Leif didn't appear to have noticed.

'The time to go to bed is when you feel tired,' he said. He gave her a warm smile. '*Got natt.*'

She answered in the same language, adding in English, 'And thanks again—for everything.'

Her '*Got natt*' to Rune elicited no more than a grunt by way of reply, but it was at least an acknowledgement. Hopefully, he was beginning to accept the situation.

Despite the overcast skies, it was still far too light for sleep to come naturally. She spent twenty minutes or so manicuring her nails, flicked through one of the magazines thoughtfully provided, then went to draw the curtains across the window in an effort to deceive her senses into believing it really was bedtime.

Terje was coming from the direction of the lake, moving with the long and easy stride of the seasoned walker. Hands thrust into trouser pockets, head bent, he seemed to be lost in thought. She wished she could only hate him again—

except that she never really had hated him, had she? The antagonism had been a defence against emotions he had aroused in her from the word go. One look, and she had been lost.

The blond head lifted suddenly, as if drawn by some invisible wire, and he looked directly at her window. It was too late to dart back, so she stayed where she was. She even managed a casual wave of a hand. From this distance it was impossible to see his expression, but he acknowledged the gesture before continuing on his way.

No matter what the limitations on his feelings where she was concerned, she would give anything to be with him tomorrow instead of Nils, she reflected despondently. Not that he would necessarily be spending the day alone, of course. In his position, and still unmarried, he would be the focus of every unattached female in the area—with Inger as a case in point.

When she did eventually sleep, it was fitfully. She was heavy-eyed in the morning, and feeling more than a little depressed. Leif was just going out of the door when she went downstairs. She wondered where he was off to. Almost certainly not a business trip on a Sunday. It couldn't be lack of opportunity that prevented him from marrying again; position aside, he was still a vitally attractive man. He must, she thought, have loved his wife a great deal.

Wearing jeans and a lightweight sweatshirt, Terje was already eating breakfast. He poured coffee for her as she took her place at the table, acknowledging her murmured thanks with an inclination of his head. The blue eyes were devoid of expression.

'Why did you run away last night?' he asked.

'I was hardly running away,' Kirsten denied, trying to sound relaxed about it. 'What would I be running from? I was tired, so I went to bed early. Don't you ever do that?'

His shrug dismissed the subject. 'What time is Nils coming for you?'

'Nine o'clock.' She hesitated, wanting to communicate her lack of enthusiasm for the arrangement, but doubting if it would make any difference. Like it or not, he couldn't object to her spending time with Nils without committing himself to a degree of involvement he obviously didn't want. She said instead, 'At least the weather improved. It looks a good day for sailing.'

'It will be,' Terje agreed.

'You're going out on your own?'

He shook his head. 'Inger will be joining me.'

The words were jerked from her. 'Why don't you marry the girl? You must know how she feels about you.'

'I could do very much worse,' he agreed on a dispassionate note. 'Unlike her brother, she's a very fine person.'

Kirsten swallowed hard on the lump in her throat. 'I'm sure she is.'

There was a car coming along the drive. It was only fifteen minutes past eight, so it was unlikely to be Nils. Terje got to his feet and moved to the door as the vehicle drew to a stop out front, returning moments later with Inger in tow. Like him, she was wearing jeans and sweatshirt, making Kirsten feel distinctly the odd man out in her well-cut beige trousers and cream silk shirt.

'*Hallo*,' greeted the newcomer politely. 'I'm sorry to interrupt your breakfast.'

Kirsten managed a smile. 'I'm only having coffee. There's plenty left in the pot, if you'd like some?'

There was an unused cup already on the table, as if in anticipation. Inger took a seat alongside Terje, and poured him a fresh cup before filling one for herself, an air of familiarity in her actions. The eyes which lifted to meet Kirsten's across the table were cool.

'You must find Norway very undeveloped compared with England.'

'I find it very beautiful,' Kirsten returned. 'More even than I expected.'

'But you prefer your homeland, of course?'

Terje was listening expressionlessly to the exchange. Kirsten kept her tone light. 'I obviously love my own country, but not to the point where I could never live anywhere else.'

'*I* could never live anywhere else but here,' stated the other girl on a note of finality. 'It's the only place I ever want to be.'

'My grandmother possibly felt the same until she met my grandfather.' This time Kirsten allowed her glance to shift momentarily to Terje, registering the thinning of his lips. 'Of course, if you marry someone of your own nationality, the problem doesn't arise.'

'Which was the mistake she made.' Terje shoved back his chair. 'Are you ready to go, Inger?'

'Of course.' She came to her feet, abandoning the coffee remaining in her cup. 'We must make the most of the breeze while it lasts. I hope you and Nils have an enjoyable day too,' she added to Kirsten.

Terje was already halfway to the door. 'Thanks,' Kirsten answered steadily. 'I'm sure we shall.'

The house seemed empty after they departed, although Berta was somewhere around. With half an hour still to go before Nils would arrive, she debated going for a walk in the grounds, but decided she was hardly dressed for tramping through damp grass.

Had things worked out the way they should, she would be the one going sailing with Terje today, she reflected hollowly. Not that it would have made any difference to the end result. In a few days she would be gone. It was a pity that she hadn't left well alone in the first place.

Nils arrived promptly on the hour, surprised but not displeased to find her alone. Devastatingly handsome in the fawn suede jacket and toning, beautifully tailored trousers, he was every girl's dreamboat, Kirsten supposed, but her heart-strings didn't even quiver.

She made an effort to be gracious when he complimented her on her own appearance. She at least owed him that much. His charm was so facile; a little of it was going to go an awful long way, she thought wryly as he put her into the passenger seat of his gleaming red sports coupé.

They spent an hour or more viewing the medieval Håkon's Hall and Rosenkrantz Tower, both beautifully restored, then took the guided tour through nine hundred years of history at Bryggen. Nils's charm might be superficial, but his knowledge of local history was anything but, Kirsten found. He could be good company when he forgot about himself.

It was well gone midday when they finally emerged from the Hanseatic museum. Bergen was awash with tourists, the harbour packed with craft of all shapes and sizes. Jutting like long and short fingers, the two piers were festooned with rubber tyres as fenders for the smaller vessels. A score of bare masts stood outlined against a sky washed clean by the sun—an image mirrored in the still waters.

'I imagine it's much more peaceful than this in winter,' Kirsten remarked, listening to the rousing strains of a Souza march played by a youth band on the waterfront. 'Do you do a lot of skiing, Nils?'

'Everyone skis,' he said. 'In winter there is little else to do.'

She cast him a glance, struck by something in his tone.

'If you find Bergen so boring, why don't you try moving to Oslo for a while?'

'The family business is here,' he said. 'Not as big and important as Brulands, of course!' The last with an acridity he made no attempt to disguise. 'They could buy us a thousand times over.'

'If you were offered a position with Brulands, would you take it?' Kirsten ventured, and saw his lip curl.

'There is little chance of that with Terje in charge. He and I are not compatible. He took you to Trondheim because we were to spend Saturday together. The engine trouble was nothing more than a ruse!'

'That's ridiculous,' she protested. 'Of course it was genuine. I was there at the harbour when he found out about it.'

'You heard someone other than Terje himself say it?'

'Well, no,' she was bound to admit. 'But it doesn't make sense that he'd go to such trouble just to keep me from seeing you.'

Nils's eyes were on her face. 'Perhaps he had other motives too. He was involved with an English girl who looked a lot like you.'

'You mean Jean?' she said.

He was taken aback for a moment. 'He told you about her?'

'Everything,' she confirmed. 'As a matter of fact, he blamed her more than you for what happened.'

'That might be what he says.' There was a pause, a subtle change of tone. 'Shall we forget about Terje? I would prefer to talk about you.'

'Can we do it over lunch?' she asked, trying not to sound totally indifferent to his advances. 'I didn't have much breakfast.'

If he recognised the stand-off he gave no sign of it. Neither did he cut down on the beguilement during the meal. Kirsten had no doubt that most women would find him utterly charismatic, but he simply left her cold.

All she could think about was Terje, wondering if he had ever made love to Inger—whether he was making love to her right now. Jealousy was soul-destroying, but she couldn't repress it. All she could do was endure it.

Nils made it just about impossible to cut the day short by outlining his plans for the afternoon. He was taking her out round the islands by motor launch, he declared. It was all arranged. Afterwards they were to have dinner at the Bellevue, which was one of Bergen's finest restaurants.

Kirsten's attempt to evade the last was rejected on the grounds that she could telephone the house and inform Berta that she wouldn't be back for *middag*, leaving her with little choice short of downright rudeness. He had obviously gone to a lot of trouble; the very least she could do was put up a pretence of enjoying it all.

In actual fact, she did to a great extent. The scenery and sparkling sea air alone made the day worthwhile. Nils drove the launch himself, well pleased when she addressed him, tongue in cheek, as Skipper. In some ways he was still immature, Kirsten thought. Like a small boy showing off.

The Bellevue turned out to be a seventeenth-century manor house on a hill overlooking the city and fjord. The views were magnificent, the food excellent and the service second to none. The meal must be costing a small fortune, Kirsten reckoned, and felt guilty for not being more appreciative of the man paying for it all. She hadn't anticipated such a concentrated effort.

It was only afterwards, when Nils suggested they go back to his apartment for a drink, that she began to suspect he might have some form of repayment in mind. It was there in his eyes, in his smile, in the way he touched her whenever the opportunity arose. His immediate reaction when she turned the offer aside on a plea of tiredness seemed to substantiate the theory, although he covered up pretty well.

Both cars were on the drive when they got to the house, indicating that father and son were home. Nils declined to come in, but was obviously determined to have some compensation for his efforts, pulling her into his arms to kiss her with a passion that was totally unwelcome. She suffered it only because she felt she was partly to blame for not making her feelings—or lack of them—clearer. Men like Nils found it difficult to believe that a woman might find them resistible.

'I'll see you tomorrow,' he said when he reluctantly released her. 'We will watch the sunrise together.'

Kirsten had little idea of what he was talking about, and wasn't about to ask. She opened the car door and slid from her seat, relieved when he made no attempt to stop her. 'Thanks for today,' she said quickly. 'It's been lovely. *Got natt*, Nils.'

She was in the house before he drove off. The men were in the living-room; she could hear their voices, the clink of glasses. She didn't want to go in, but it would be discourteous, she decided, to go straight upstairs without at least saying goodnight.

Terje was seated with his back to her, Rune fast asleep in his customary chair, Leif facing the door. 'Come and have a drink with us,' he invited easily, getting to his feet. 'What would you like?'

'*Akevitt*, please,' she said, relinquishing any idea of a quick departure. She could hardly start pleading tiredness again.

Terje gave her a measured scrutiny as she took a seat opposite. He was wearing trousers and shirt now, she noted. 'How did the sailing go?' she asked brightly.

'Very well,' he said. 'How was your day?'

'Fine.'

Leif handed her a glass, then resumed his seat. 'So where did Nils take you?' he asked conversationally

'Just about everywhere,' she acknowledged. 'We had dinner at the Bellevue.'

'He was certainly out to impress,' commented Terje drily. 'How did you like it?'

'Very much.' Kirsten made an effort to infuse some degree of enthusiasm into her voice. 'It's a lovely place.' She added to Leif, 'I phoned to let Berta know I wouldn't be here for *middag*.'

'Yes,' he said, 'she told me. It was thoughtful of you.'

Rune awoke with a jerk, muttering under his breath as he registered her presence. He levered himself stiffly to his feet, standing for a moment to steady himself before making slowly to the door. Neither son nor grandson offered to assist him, although both, Kirsten noted, kept an eye on his progress. The time when the old man's pride could no longer support him had to be close. It was possible, she reflected, that he would simply give up the ghost when that day finally came.

'I must apologise for my father's manner towards you,' proffered Leif, catching her eye.

'You don't need to,' she said. 'It must be difficult for him. After all, he's the only one who knows what really happened sixty years ago.'

'*Was* the only one,' Leif corrected. 'I persuaded him to tell me the whole story while we were alone this evening.'

So Terje hadn't been home all that long himself, came the fleeting thought before she took in the full substance of what Leif had said. She looked at him questioningly. 'Am I allowed to hear it?'

He inclined his head, waiting a brief moment as if to

gather his thoughts before launching forth. 'It appears that your grandmother was pregnant. While that may not mean a great deal in this day and age, it meant disgrace for the whole family name in my father's day. Had the father been Norwegian, the marriage would have taken place immediately, but an English sailor was another matter. Arrangements were made to send Kirsten away until after the birth, and have the child adopted, but she chose to go with her lover instead. After that, she was disowned her name struck from the family bible.'

Kirsten felt torn two ways. On the one hand it was good to know the truth at last, on the other she was sad at the thought of what her namesake must have suffered, not only then but for so many years afterwards. Her father had been born a whole year after the marriage took place, so it seemed that the pregnancy had not gone full term. Unless dates had been deliberately altered, that was.

'I doubt if it would have been regarded as any less of a scandal in England at that time either,' she said, shelving the thought. 'She must have gone through so much!'

'She chose her own course,' said Terje, jerking her head round towards him.

'Meaning she deserved everything she got, I suppose?'

The blue eyes regarded her dispassionately. 'Meaning that she paid the consequences of her actions. If it turned out to be the wrong choice, then that was unfortunate.'

'I'm not suggesting that she made the wrong choice,' Kirsten said tautly. 'I just don't think it was right to cast her out like a pariah!'

'Of course it wasn't right,' said Leif. 'But the conventions of the day allowed no other course. Does it make any difference who was most at fault?'

'Not really,' Kirsten was bound to acknowledge. She

added tentatively, 'What about Rune? Does he still feel the same?'

Leif made a wry gesture. 'I'm afraid he's too old and too stubborn to give way now.'

'And deserves to be left in peace.' Terje spoke with authority. 'You have the detail, so let that be enough.'

'As I can't speak the language, I can hardly badger him for more,' Kirsten responded, resenting his tone. 'I wouldn't, anyway.'

She drained her glass and set it down with a small thud, then came sharply to her feet. The room seemed to sway around her for a moment; she stumbled against the edge of the chair and would have collapsed into it again if Terje hadn't leapt up and taken hold of her.

'Never down *akevitt* in one gulp if you're not accustomed to it,' he advised with irony. 'Where were you intending to go?'

'Bed,' she said indistinctly. 'I'm all right now, thanks. It was getting up too fast, that's all.'

She scarcely knew whether to be glad or sorry when he released her, although with Leif in the room he was hardly going to be making any amorous advances. His very touch made her quiver, and she was sure he knew it. If only *she* knew how to get through the barrier he had erected.

She made her escape without further mishap, leaving the two men to finish their drinks in peace. While preparing for bed, she went over the story Leif had told her, and came to the conclusion that it was time to put the whole thing aside. It would have been nice to feel that Rune was ready to do the same, but it obviously wasn't to be.

Tonight, with little or no cloud in the sky, the light took even longer to fade. She dozed off eventually, but was wide awake again at two, lying there tossing and turning for a further half-hour before decided enough was enough. It wasn't fully dark even now, and the room felt stuffy. She could have opened a window, but she needed more than that. There was a hint of claustrophobia in the way she felt.

Slipping on a wrap, she made her way downstairs, passing through the silent house to emerge on to the glass-enclosed rear porch with its waiting chairs and misty mountain views. Dressed the way she was, it would be too cool to wander outside at this hour, she knew, but this was the next best thing.

What she hadn't anticipated was to find Terje there before her. Wearing a towelling robe and with leather slippers on his feet, he was reclining in a chair with his feet up on another.

'I think we played this scene already,' he said softly.

'Do you do this often?' Kirsten asked, finding her voice at last.

'Only when I find sleep evading me for some reason,' he returned. 'What about you?'

'I couldn't sleep either.'

His smile was ironic. 'Too much of it last night, perhaps?'

She refused to be drawn. 'Perhaps. It's a lovely night, isn't it?'

'They all are when the weather allows it. Hopefully, it will last through tomorrow too.'

'What exactly happens tomorrow?' she asked.

'In the cities, we celebrate the shortest night of the year with bonfires and fireworks, and dancing in the streets, although many prefer to take picnic baskets and blankets and head for their boats or skerry cottages. We'll be spending the night as we always do at our own cottage up the coast from here. Rune would have it no other way.' He paused briefly. 'The Torvunds will be joining us as usual. Did Nils not mention it?'

'He did say something.'

Terje was silent for a long moment, expression enigmatic. When he spoke again it was on a different note. 'Why did you go to bed with me, Kirsten?'

Her heart jerked painfully. It took everything she had to keep her voice from reflecting the turmoil inside her. 'For the same reason, I suppose, that you had. As you said yourself, lust isn't confined to the male.'

His smile lacked humour. 'So I did.' There was another pause, another change of tone. 'Perhaps we should continue to indulge our mutual passions while the opportunity still exists.'

Kirsten gazed at him in torment, fighting the instinctive desire to say yes. Making love with Terje again could only serve to intensify the pain of eventual parting.

'I don't think that would be a good idea,' she got out.

'It probably isn't,' he agreed. 'But it's what we both want.'

He got up from the chair, moving purposefully to where she stood by the inner door to take her unresistingly in his arms. Blood singing, heart hammering wildly against the wall of her chest, she could do no other than respond to the sheer hunger in his lips. It might be a long way from the depth of emotion she wanted from him, but it was love of a kind. If she turned away from it, what was she left with?

'Let's go inside,' he said softly, and she knew she hadn't the strength of mind to say no. Live for today, she told herself as he turned her back into the house.

He took her to his room. Probably, that part of her mind still functioning rationally suggested, because his father had the room next to hers. Kissing her, he deftly removed her wrap and pyjama-top, then pushed the silky trousers down over her hips until they fell smoothly to the floor. Still kissing her, he shrugged off the towelling robe and drew her to him, smoothing both hands down the length of her back to pressure her into closer proximity with his heat and hardness.

'You see what you do to me,' he murmured.

'No more than you do to me,' she whispered back, and he gave a low laugh.

'But not so obviously. That's a woman's advantage.'

He brought his hands up again to slide them about her neck, fingers seeking the sensitive spots just behind her earlobes with a delicacy that sent tremor after tremor through her body. She put her lips to the strong brown column of his throat, tasting salt on his skin as she kissed her way down to the first tickle of his chest hair, allowing her hands to be her eyes. He was so beautifully built, the muscle in shoulders and upper arms firmly defined, chest broad and strong, tapering to a waist that bore no single inch of surplus flesh, hips flat and hard, abdomen as taut as a drum.

He drew in his breath as she found him, lifting her head to seek her mouth again with a passion that lit an answering flame in her. She went down beneath him on to the bed at her back, wrapping her limbs about him as he drove into her; matching each powerful, urgent stroke with one of her own until she could no longer hold out. The cry wrenched from her lips was following immediately by Terje's deep, gasping groan, and for a brief moment she bore the full brunt of his weight as the use went from him.

Not that she wanted him to move. Pinioned there beneath him, she felt at peace with the whole world. She said his name tremulously, lovingly, uncaring of what she might be giving away.

It was like losing a part of herself when he eased away from her, even though he didn't go far. Lying on his side, supported on one elbow, he leaned over her to kiss her, his free hand resting lightly on her hipbone.

'How do you feel?' he asked softly.

Much as she wanted to, Kirsten couldn't find the courage to say the words. 'Good,' she said inadequately. '*Very, very good!*'

Terje put a finger to her lips, his smile dry. 'It's unnecessary to boost my ego any further than you already did by showing yourself as eager as I am myself to continue our affair.'

'Affair?' Her voice sounded rough.

'Two people indulging a mutual need. Isn't that the word for it?'

'I suppose it is,' she managed. 'Are you suggesting that we go on indulging the need until I go home on Friday?'

'Unless you have some objection?' He waited a moment, his regard narrowing a fraction. 'Do you?'

If she said yes, she would spend the next four days and nights regretting it, Kirsten knew. Caution was for the cautious; she was going for what she could get.

'No,' she said huskily.

Something leapt in the blue eyes. Rolling on to his back, he pulled her over him, bringing her head down to his with a hand at her nape. She kissed him back feverishly, wantonly, aware of his regeneration. His hands fastened on her hips, lifting her and fitting her to him, making her gasp as he penetrated her by slow degrees until their bodies rested tightly together; filling her with his hardness.

Eyes closed, back arching, Kirsten allowed her instinct free rein. Her movement was slow and sensuous, bringing the breath hissing between his clenched teeth. She was in charge, and loving it, but not for long. Grasping her about the waist, he turned her under him in one powerful surge, eyes like blue flames as he took command, his very dominance exciting her beyond the point of any control at all.

She must have fallen asleep for a minute or two after that soaring climax. When she opened her eyes again Terje had gone, although sounds from the *en-suite* bathroom told her where.

The heartache she was storing up for herself by doing this was going to be with her for a long time, she knew. If she could only convince Terje to trust her, he might realise for himself how ideally they belonged together, but it would take time she didn't have to undo the damage Jean had done.

All the same, she would try, she resolved. Even if she didn't fully succeed before she boarded the ferry on Friday, she could at least leave the way open for a return.

She was lying facing the bathroom door when Terje emerged. Unselfconscious in his masculine nudity, he set her pulses racing all over again as he moved towards her. Sliding under the covering duvet, he kissed her lightly on the lips before turning her about to draw her up closely against him, his hand seeking her breast.

'Sleep,' he said softly.

He went to sleep almost immediately; she could tell that from his breathing. The intimacy of the embrace held her in thrall for quite some time longer before she finally succumbed herself.

CHAPTER EIGHT

FIRST TO sleep, Terje was also first awake. By the time Kirsten opened her eyes, he was already up and dressed.

This was what marriage would be like, she thought, watching him through her lashes as he moved about the room. If only she could wave a magic wand and make it true!

As if sensing her observation, he came over to the bed, looking down at her with a reminiscent smile on his lips. 'You were sleeping like a baby,' he said. 'I had no heart to awaken you earlier.' He bent to kiss her on the tip of her nose in a gesture close enough to tenderness to bring warmth to her heart. 'I'll see you later.'

It was only then that she realised it was now Monday and he would be going in to the office. Not just today either, but all week, limiting their time together to mere hours rather than days.

Pure instinct drove her to slide her arms up about his neck before he could lift away again, and hold him there for a lingering kiss of her own. His response was instant and gratifying, but he didn't allow it to get out of hand.

'I have to go,' he declared. 'I have a busy day scheduled.' A hand came up to smooth the lock of hair from her cheek. 'I'm leaving you my car. Just remember that we drive on the right here.'

Kirsten eased herself upright as he went from the room, determined to look on the positive side. There were still plenty of places she hadn't visited. Troldhaugen, for one. It was good of Terje to offer her use of the car. Obviously he had taken it for granted that she held a licence. Thankfully, the car had automatic transmission. It was enough to be driving on the wrong side of the road without having to contend with a right-hand gear-box too.

First, though, she had to get back to her own room. It wouldn't do for Berta to find her here. Her pyjamas and wrap were laid neatly over a chair-back. She put them on and went to the door, opening it a fraction to listen for any sound of movement in the immediate vicinity before continuing on through.

Rune's bedroom door was opposite, but he would still be asleep at this hour, she reassured herself. Even if he were awake, he would naturally assume it was Terje himself leaving. As a guest in the house, her behaviour left a whole lot to be desired as it was, she conceded ruefully. Leif himself would be unlikely to approve of the situation–and who could blame him?

All the same, she knew she wouldn't be saying no to whatever opportunity she had to be with Terje during the time left to her.

The two men had already left by the time she went down. Berta brought in fresh coffee and departed again before Kirsten had a chance to apologise for her tardiness. And there, she thought, went another who would be happy to see the back of her on Friday!

There was still no sign of Rune when she left the house at ten. It was cooler today, with a promise of rain again in the cloud piling up on the horizon. She had little difficulty in finding Troldhaugen, although it was already awash with visitors by the time she got there. Too many for more than a cursory look around the lovely old clapboard house with its well-preserved contents.

The Fantoft stave church was also overrun, but she could still stand back and admire the pagoda-like symmetry of its design. For a building made entirely from wooden staves to have come through eight hundred years with so little obvious deterioration was almost unbelievable.

A couple walking past with their arms about each other made her yearn all the more for Terje to be here with her. If he asked her to stay on beyond Friday she would do it, she knew. Only she doubted if he would.

With the Midsummer celebrations already under way, parking in Bergen itself proved something of a problem. Eventually she found a place on one of the back-streets, and walked down to Strandgaten to take a look at the shops.

Prices here really were astronomical, she reflected, studying the tickets on a rack of shoes outside one store and doing quick calculations. Forty-eight pounds for a pair of simple black pumps was hardly her idea of a sales bargain! She had to admit, though, that it was only the foreigners who looked askance at the cost. The Norwegians themselves had incomes on a par.

Torvunds was one of the largest stores. She went in purely out of curiosity. There were three floors to the place, and a superb range of goods on display. A thriving business too, she judged, from the number of customers milling about. Nils should count himself fortunate to be part of it.

She somehow hadn't anticipated running into him on the shop floor. Stepping off the final escalator to see him talking with another man some few feet away, she looked round swiftly for some means of escape, but it was too late because he had already seen her. She tried her best to look welcoming when he broke off his conversation and came over to where she stood.

'*Hallo*!' he greeted her. 'This is sooner than I hoped for!'

'I was just passing,' she said lamely.

'At just the right time,' he responded. 'Give me a moment to tell my secretary, and we will go for lunch.'

It was on the tip of Kirsten's tongue to claim a previous arrangement, but he was gone before she could frame the words. An engagement with whom, in any case? Nils was only too well aware that she knew no one in Bergen outside of the Brulands family, and would be equally well aware that Terje was otherwise engaged. It would only be for an hour or so, she consoled herself.

He took her to an Italian restaurant called Michelangelo. The atmosphere was authentic, the food too, although Kirsten would have preferred some simpler fare at this hour of the day. She felt guilty to be here at all considering the way she felt—or didn't feel—about Nils. He was not only wasting his money, he was wasting his time.

'You really shouldn't go to such expense,' she protested over coffee, mentally totting up the cost of the meal they had just eaten. 'You must have spent a small fortune on me yesterday.'

'I can afford it,' he returned with a hint of asperity. 'I may not be able to match Terje's income, but you need not concern yourself.'

Kirsten gave an inward sigh. 'I didn't mean to suggest you couldn't afford it. I just feel I'm taking advantage of your generosity, that's all.'

Nils smiled, apparently mollified by the explanation. 'You are worth every *krona*. Tomorrow evening I'll take you to a nightclub.'

'It's nice of you to ask me,' she said swiftly, doing her best to sound suitably regretful, 'but I'm afraid I already made other arrangements.'

'With Terje?' His tone had shortened again.

'Yes.'

'You realise that he and Inger have an involvement?'

She said carefully, 'I'm not sure what you mean by involvement. I know they see one another.'

'They do a great deal more than that.' His lip curled. 'She expects him to marry her.'

'But you don't?'

'No. He's just using her because she's my sister, and I'm the one who took Jean away from him.'

'I don't think we should be discussing this,' said Kirsten thickly.

'You mean you don't like hearing it.' His mouth narrowed as he studied her face. 'He obviously wasted little time with you as well!'

The colour came and went in her cheeks. 'I think I'd better go,' she said.

Nils put out a staying hand as she half rose from her seat, his expression taut. 'You are drawing attention.'

Conscious of it already, she reluctantly subsided again, only too well aware that her reaction to the remark had served to confirm its intimation. 'Let's just forget it,' she said briefly.

For a moment there was a disturbing expression in the pale blue eyes, then he gave a dismissive shrug and turned his attention back to his coffee, leaving her to do the same.

He made no attempt to detain her when they got outside again. Whatever his intentions had been, it was apparent that he had no further interest in pursuing them. She refused to believe that Terje would play Inger along for the reasons Nils had stated, because it made no sense, but if Inger really felt that she had reason to anticipate his marrying her, then there was more to their relationship than he had intimated.

She was the one being used, she thought bleakly as she made her way back to the car, and it stopped right here before she made a fool of herself altogether.

The cloud had begun to disperse after shedding a couple

of showers, giving promise of a fine evening and night to come. She spent an hour or so touring Old Bergen with its emotive glimpses of the city her grandmother would have known, returning to the house at the same time that Leif and Terje arrived home at four o'clock.

'We're to leave at seven,' Terje confirmed in answer to her query, as his father disappeared indoors. 'The cottage is no more than a forty-minute journey from here. Berta will have *middag* ready at five instead of six.' He gave her a measuring look, as if registering some difference in her. 'What did you do with yourself today?'

'I went to Troldhaugen and Fantoft, then into town to see Old Bergen,' she responded. 'It was good of you to let me have the car.'

'I found it no problem to travel with my father. Is anything wrong?' he added. 'You seem. . .distracted.'

Disturbed would be closer the mark, she thought, and decided to get it over with.

'I came to a decision while I was out,' she said, not looking at him. 'I think it's time we called a halt.'

'Just like that?' His voice was quiet, though far from soft. 'The doubts were far from apparent this morning?'

'I wasn't thinking straight this morning,' she claimed. 'This is your father's house, and I'm abusing his hospitality.'

They had reached the hallway. Terje stopped moving, eyes penetrating her defences. 'It's my home too.'

'Then it shouldn't be,' she rejoined hardily. 'Not if you want to live the bachelor life.'

'You mean if I had a place of my own you would be happy to continue our association?'

'The word,' she said, trying to sound blasé about it, 'is affair. And yes, I suppose it might make a difference.'

'Only might?'

'Would, then,' she substituted. 'Only you haven't, so it's immaterial.'

'Terje!' Leif had emerged from the living-room and was standing a few feet away. For the first time in Kirsten's presence, he addressed his son in Norwegian, causing a sudden premonition of disaster as she listened to the clipped accents and watched the younger man's expression change.

Terje gave a terse nod, and went into the living-room, closing the door in his wake. Kirsten looked at Leif uncertainly, hoping against hope that her instincts were telling her wrong.

'Is Rune ill?' she asked, unable to think of anything else to say.

'Not ill, just very troubled,' came the measured response. 'He heard you and Terje come upstairs last night, and knows that the two of you spent the rest of the night together.'

Kirsten bit her lip, feeling the hot colour flood her face. 'I'm sorry,' she said huskily. 'It just. . .happened.'

'It often does,' he returned without censure. 'I sensed the attraction between the two of you from the moment you met.'

She gazed at him wordlessly for a moment, unable to believe what he appeared to be saying. 'You don't. . .disapprove?'

The smile was faint. 'You are of an age where such decisions are entirely your own affair.'

'It's your house.'

His shoulders lifted in a brief shrug. 'Two years ago, when my wife died, I asked Terje to move back here purely out of self-interest because I needed his companionship, without giving any thought at all to the limitations such a move must place on his lifestyle. With you right here in the house, and obviously sharing the same feelings, what happened was almost inevitable. What I might have asked from you both was a little more discretion. Rune's hearing is excellent for his age, and his sleep fitful.'

'I'm sorry,' Kirsten said again. 'I really am, Leif. I don't make a habit of this kind of thing.'

'I had no thought that you did,' he returned. The blue eyes, so like those of his son, held an odd expression. 'Which leads me to believe that your feelings for my son may be more than just a physical attraction. Am I right?'

There was only one answer she could make without destroying every last vestige of self-respect. If it were repeated to Terje himself, then she would just have to live with it. 'You could be,' she said softly.

'Enough to contemplate marriage with him?'

The shock of it gripped her by the throat. She stared at him wide-eyed for several seconds before the spasm passed.

'What are you talking about?' she got out. 'There's no question of—'

'Rune has had all day to reach his conclusions,' Leif interrupted. 'Your grandfather had the decency to marry his sister after besmirching her, therefore Terje can do no less if the family honour is to be upheld.'

'But that's ridiculous!' Kirsten's thoughts were in absolute turmoil.

'Ridiculous or not, that is what he will be telling Terje he has to do.'

Her laugh sounded brittle. 'He's hardly likely to agree to it!'

'If he does, will you be prepared to do the same?'

'The question won't arise,' she said desperately. 'The whole idea is preposterous! He'll make Rune see that for himself.'

'Once set, my father's mind is not easily swerved from

its purpose,' Leif responded drily. 'You must know that already.'

'What about you?' she asked. 'Surely you don't agree with him too?'

'He's an old man, with little time left,' came the level reply. 'His peace of mind is important to me–as I trust it is to Terje also. You came here to achieve family unity. What better way could there be?'

'I'd like to go to my room,' she said unsteadily. 'I can't cope with this.'

'But think about it,' he urged.

She could hear the sound of voices from the living-room as she mounted the stairs, one of them raised. She wouldn't need to think about it, she assured herself numbly; Terje was obviously seeing to that. He was right to be angry too. Shotgun weddings went out with the Dark Ages.

She was lying on the bed gazing blindly at the ceiling when the knock came on her door some untold time later. It opened before she had a chance to make any response, jerking every nerve-ending in her body as Terje came in and closed it again behind him.

'We have to talk,' he said.

'What is there to talk about?' she managed with creditable calm, sitting up. 'I imagine you told your grandfather exactly the same thing I told your father.'

She waited for the anticipated reply, heart beating a painful tattoo against the wall of her chest when it failed to materialise immediately. Standing there, hands thrust deep into trouser pockets, expression grimly controlled, he was all too obviously at war within himself.

'I understand 'Far already told you what Rune expects of us,' he said at length. 'How do you feel about it?'

'The same way you do, of course,' she said. 'You surely told him it was out of the question!'

'He refuses to accept it.'

'He has to accept it!' She said it with force. 'He doesn't have any choice.'

'But he does have a heart that may stop any time if put under strain.' Terje made the statement unemotionally. 'He was becoming too agitated just now when I was attempting to reason with him. I would hate to be responsible for his premature death.'

Kirsten gazed at him uncertainly, eyes dark. 'What are you saying exactly?'

'That I had to stop contesting him before he suffered an attack.'

'You mean you told him you'd do as he wants?'

'I said I would talk to you about it.'

Her voice sounded as if it was coming from a long distance away. 'So you talked to me.'

The blue eyes didn't flicker. 'The idea has its merits. We already established a basis.'

'Not for marriage.' She was struggling to retain some degree of rationality. 'We've only known each other a few days. What kind of basis is that?'

'Enough to build on.' He studied her for a moment, then took his hands from his pockets to move purposefully towards her. 'Like this.'

She made no move to evade him for the simple reason that her limbs wouldn't work. Reaching over the foot of the bed, he drew her up to him, finding her mouth in a kiss that sent tremor after tremor through her. It would be so easy to just go along with it all, she thought shakily. Too easy. If Terje married her simply because his grandfather commanded it, nothing would ever be clear between them.

'I can't,' she whispered painfully. 'It isn't enough!'

'Then we have to make it enough,' he said with purpose.

'Or would you prefer to be responsible for what may happen if you refuse?'

'You're putting me in a cleft-stick,' she protested. 'That's not fair!'

'I have no choice. If Rune is to reach the century he always hoped for, he has to be indulged.' He paused, his mouth taking on a slant. 'As I'm the last in our immediate line, it's also time that I produced a son.'

Kirsten drew back her head to look at him, still unable to believe he was really serious. 'But the bloodline wouldn't be pure any longer. Surely Rune wouldn't want that?'

'Foolproof contraception was unheard of in his day. He probably considers it too late already—the same way it was with your grandmother by the time the affair was discovered.'

'If that's his main concern, you can assure him that there's no danger where I'm concerned,' she said.

'I doubt if he would take your word for it.'

She was silent for a long moment, torn in half by the conflict going on inside her. If she said yes she would be gaining both husband and lover, but she would still be minus his love. Could she accept that?

'What about Inger?' she asked thickly, and saw his expression undergo a subtle alteration.

'Inger has no relevance to the situation.'

'She's in love with you,' Kirsten protested. 'You must know that.'

'It has no bearing,' he reiterated. 'You're the one I'm to marry.'

'Only if I say yes!'

'Then say it.' He drew her to him again, kissing her with a passion bordering on anger. 'Say it!'

'All right!' The words were dragged from her by the

sheer force of his will. She didn't have a choice, she told herself. Rune's very life might depend on his getting his way. Could she risk robbing him of whatever years he had remaining? 'All right,' she repeated more softly.

There was more resignation than triumph in the vivid eyes, she judged, but it was too late now to start changing her mind. Given the time, she could make him love her, she thought determinedly. She *had* to make him love her! She kissed him hungrily, concentrating on the more immediate emotions, heartened by his response. At least he still wanted her. She could manage on that for the present.

He took her swiftly, almost fiercely, as if anger still played a certain part, gentling only at the last when he pressed his lips to her temple where the hair clung damply; murmuring something in his own language that she couldn't catch. Words trembled on her own lips, but she couldn't bring herself to say them. All in good time, she told herself. All in good time.

'It must be almost five,' she murmured softly instead.

'And we still have to put Rune's mind at rest,' Terje agreed, releasing her. 'I hope you won't expect too much from him. It will still take time for him to adjust, even though it was he who insisted that I did the right thing by you.'

'I'll try to be tolerant,' Kirsten promised. 'Do we have to tell him together?'

He pressed himself upright, reaching for the clothing so hastily discarded. 'You have to face him some time.'

'What on earth do I tell my parents?' she asked in sudden realisation, coming sharply upright herself.

Terje paused in contemplation for a moment, brows drawn together. 'We just tell them we're to be married. There is no other way.'

She said in relief, 'You'll come with me?'

'I think I have to,' he said. 'I imagine your parents will want the wedding to take place in England. How long will you need to make arrangements?'

'I don't know.' Kirsten was only just beginning to consider the ramifications. It would be difficult enough to tell them about the marriage plans to start with; a hastily arranged wedding was totally out of the question. 'Three months, perhaps.'

'Three months!' Terje shook his head. 'Too long.'

For him, she wondered, or for Rune?

'I'll need to give notice at work.' she pointed out. 'They'll have to find themselves another trained hygienist.'

'And in the meantime we stay apart?'

She looked back at him helplessly. 'What other course is there?'

'A swiftly arranged marriage right here in Bergen,' he said on a decisive note. 'That way Rune can be assured.'

So could she, came the fleeting thought, hastily put aside. 'I can't spring a *fait accompli* like that on my parents. They'd be devastated!'

'They would get over it. You're old enough to make your own decisions in your own time'.

'Except that it isn't my decision, is it?' she reminded him. 'It's Rune's.'

Some flicker of an unreadable expression crossed the lean features. 'All the more reason to settle the matter quickly.'

'I can't,' she said. 'I really can't, Terje.'

For a moment it seemed that he was going to continue the argument, then he shrugged. 'So we compromise. A civil ceremony in England should take no longer to arrange than here.'

A register office wedding would be almost as hard for her mother to accept as the fact of the marriage itself, Kirsten knew. How did she begin to explain such extreme haste without shocking them both to the core by telling them the truth? It simply couldn't be done.

'It won't work,' she said. 'We might reduce the time element, but it has to be in church, with the banns called in the customary manner. That means no less than three weeks, even if the vicar can fit it in.'

This was all so unreal, she thought bemusedly as she waited for Terje's response. To be sitting here discussing wedding plans with a man she hadn't even known a bare week! It would be different if they had both fallen madly in love, and couldn't wait to be together. Her mother was a romantic at heart; she might accept that scenario. It would take effort from both sides to convince her, though.

'If it must be, it must be,' he conceded. 'I'll go and tell Rune now, while you dress.'

He made no attempt to kiss her again, but simply smiled briefly and left. Kirsten galvanised herself into action, aware that she had just ten minutes before *middag*. She wasn't looking forward to seeing the old man. He might be insisting on the marriage taking place, but his attitude towards her was hardly going to be improved by his knowledge of what she had done. It promised to be anything but a comfortable meal.

She delayed until the last possible moment before going downstairs, to find the three men already seated at the table. Leif gave her a reassuring smile as she slid into her chair, but Rune simply looked through her. Without the language, she had no hope of ever achieving a breakthrough, she thought. That had to be a first priority.

'It's understandable that you would wish the marriage to take place in England,' said Leif. 'And your parents must be told as soon as possible, of course. Unfortunately, Terje has commitments he must fulfil before he accompanies you, so you may as well take the ferry as you intended on Friday. In the meantime, perhaps you should telephone your parents.'

Kirsten shook her head. 'I'd rather wait and tell them face to face. It's going to be enough of a shock as it is.'

'Yes, I can see that. I shall accompany Terje, of course, when the time comes, but if there is anything I can do in the meantime I will be only too pleased.' He paused reflectively, looking at his son. 'You will plan to come straight back here afterwards?'

'Without a honeymoon?' Terje sounded ironic. 'I think we might take a few days to accustom ourselves.'

'But of course,' Leif agreed without haste. 'As long as you need. Selvi will take over your affairs. He turned his attention back to Kirsten. 'I look forward to having you as a daughter-in-law.'

'*Takk.*' She could think of nothing more to say. It was the first time it had really dawned on her that Norway would be her home once she was married to Terje, although she didn't find that thought too daunting. There was a part of her that had always belonged here. If this marriage were a normal one, she would be happy to live anywhere, but it wouldn't be happening at all without the outmoded dictum of one old man.

Obviously frustrated by his inability to understand what was being said, the latter drew his son's attention with a querulous demand. Kirsten hardened her heart against him, looking away to find Terje watching her with an odd expression in his eyes. She managed to smile at him, but it was a puny effort, eliciting little more of a response. He felt the same way she did, she was sure, but he wouldn't risk defying his grandfather. Any refusal to comply could only come from her, and she had already given her word.

She put on jeans and a sweater for the trip, and took

along a windcheater just in case it turned really cool. It was
apparently the tradition for everyone to stay up and watch
the sunrise.

With Berta accompanying them, it was necessary to take
both cars. Seated at Terje's side as he followed the other
vehicle down the drive, Kirsten wondered if the Torvunds
were to be told the news. Inger was going to be badly hurt,
regardless of where and when, but even more so if she had
to hear it this way.

'What are you thinking?' asked Terje after a moment or
two, glancing her way. 'Are you having doubts?'

'Of course,' she said. 'We're doing what we're doing for
all the wrong reasons.'

'And what would you consider the right ones?'

She kept her gaze on the view beyond the windscreen.
'Love, for one thing, I suppose.'

He didn't answer right away. When he did it was without
particular inflexion. 'We have everything else.'

'You mean we're good together in bed?'

His lips quirked suddenly. 'Extremely good!'

'But we still have to learn to live together.'

'So do all newly-weds. We won't be staying with 'Far
and Rune. We'll have a home of our own.'

'Your father is going to miss your company,' she remarked. 'I imagine Rune's conversation is fairly limited.'

'He can still hold an audience with his folk tales, but
yes, I suppose it is,' Terje agreed. 'However, it won't be
long before the house has a new mistress—and Margot can
certainly converse.'

Kirsten looked at him swiftly. 'Your father is getting
married again?'

'Yes. Although they have yet to set a date for the wedding. She has a business of her own to run.' He paused,

his expression contemplative. 'Would you want to continue your own work?'

So many things to consider, and so little time to do it in, she thought. 'The question is, would I be able to?'

'We have dentists here in Bergen.'

'But you'd prefer a non-working wife?' she hazarded.

His shrug made light of the question. 'I hadn't given it any consideration.'

He hadn't given marriage itself any consideration until this afternoon, she thought ruefully. Not with her, at any rate.

'If this hadn't happened, *might* you have married Inger some day?' she asked because she couldn't help herself.

'I might have done a lot of things.' His voice had become a little brusque. 'Forget about Inger.'

He wouldn't deny it because he couldn't deny it, she surmised, and felt a sudden aching sympathy with the girl she had robbed.

CHAPTER NINE

THE COTTAGE was actually two skerries knocked into one to form a living area and two bedrooms, with a kitchen and bathroom built on at the back. The furnishings were simple, the whole place clean as a whistle.

The view from the doorstep was superb: a seascape scattered with islands, a coastline like a handful of finger knuckles. Standing there feasting her eyes, Kirsten could envisage spending long summer weekends roaming the cliffs and beaches, the winter ones skiing the inland slopes. With calor gas the only source of power, apart from the wood-burning iron stove, conditions were primitive compared with where they had just come from, but the lack of electricity was a small price to pay for the sheer freedom of spirit.

'Most Norwegian families have their skerry,' said Terje, joining her. 'Some abandon the city altogether during the summer months, although the men have to commute, of course.'

'Do you ever spend weekends up here yourself?' she asked.

'Sometimes.'

'Alone?'

'Not always.' He sounded a little remote, as if his thoughts weren't fully on what he was saying. 'The Torvunds are late this year.'

As if on cue came the sound of an engine, closely followed by another. The two cars pulled in behind their own vehicles at the bottom of the narrow track that was the only access from the road.

At first glance it appeared that Nils and Inger had shared transport, but the girl with him was a stranger, Kirsten realised, as the two approached. Another blonde, of course.

Nils introduced his guest as Karin Vinsevik. His secretary, Kirsten was later to learn. He seemed to have recovered from his lunchtime rancour, although the smile he gave her was a trifle on the cool side.

Inger had travelled with her parents. Seeing the way her eyes lit up when she saw Terje, Kirsten had to turn away. Even if Terje wasn't madly in love with the girl, she would make a far more suitable wife for him than she herself could ever be. They shared the same interests, the same background.

Rune would have approved of the match, she had little doubt. In insisting on *this* marriage, he could finish up ruining three lives. Surely he wouldn't want that? He should be made to understand that today's codes of behaviour were totally different from those of his day and age, and leave them to make their own choices. Without love to back it, Terje's desire for her would wane. She would prefer to lose him altogether than live with a man who no longer even wanted her.

Packed by Berta, the two picnic baskets were full to overflowing. A table was dragged from the cottage and the *koldtbord* laid out on it, together with the beer and *akevitt*. There would be coffee or tea later on for those who wanted it. The Norwegians, Kirsten reflected, did nothing by halves!

Still full from *middag* herself, she could find little appetite for another feast, although the food was scheduled to last out most of the night, judging from the quantity.

An armchair had been brought out for Rune, but the rest of them disported themselves on the grass, Berta included. Primed with *akevitt*, the housekeeper was more relaxed than Kirsten had even seen her, giggling like a schoolgirl over some remark Leif made to her.

It seemed strange that the woman he was to marry was missing from the assembly. Unless she had family of her own she preferred to be with on this one night of the year, of course. Terje would have been moving out to a place of his own again anyway when the two of them were married, she assumed.

She felt very much out of things when Rune began to relate his folk stories. Terje attempted to translate for her, but had to stop when his grandfather glowered across at him, low-toned though his voice had been.

'You'll soon learn the language once you're here,' he assured her when the story-telling was given a rest and conversation became general again. 'You can take proper tuition in order to hurry it along, if you feel you must. Apart from Rune, you're unlikely to meet up with anyone unable to speak any English at all. He never learned because it wasn't compulsory in his schooldays, and—'

'And he has a built-in resistance to anything English,' she finished for him. 'Which makes it even more difficult to understand why he would take the option he has, rather than simply insist that I leave.'

'I can't claim to understand the way his mind works either,' Terje acknowledged.

'He despises me!' Some deep-down sense of injustice was surfacing, along with some other emotion not yet defined. Her voice took on a sudden dissonant note. 'In his view, I'm just a slut! Why would he want his only grandson to marry a slut?'

'Stop saying that!' Terje spoke with authority, jaw set. 'If you were a *sjuske*, what would that make me?'

'It isn't the same for a man, is it?' she said with bitterness. 'It never was—even in your grandfather's day. You could make love with as many women as you like without being regarded as anything worse than a bit of a philanderer. And probably have,' she added half under her breath.

'I think that's enough!' Terje was angry and showing it, face grim. 'I don't know why you suddenly feel the need to say these things, but I've no intention of defending myself against them.'

Kirsten knew why. Jealousy pure and simple. It had been building up in her ever since the Torvunds had arrived. The only former lover she was bothered about was Inger. She was watching the two of them right now. Watching, and wondering.

'Isn't it about time you told Inger the truth, and put her out of her misery?' she said tersely. 'Or do you intend leaving it until after we're married?'

'I'll choose my own time!' He paused, obviously fighting to control his temper. When he spoke again it was in less volatile tones. 'Why are you being this way?'

Kirsten drew in a ragged breath. 'I suppose,' she said, 'because I'm just beginning to fully appreciate what I'm being asked—no, *told*—to do. I have my own life back home. Why should I be expected to settle down here simply to satisfy one man's convoluted notions of honour—a man who refused even to acknowledge his own sister's death? If you stopped pandering to him he might be better for it.'

'He's eighty-four!' The tone was a whiplash.

She had gone too far to back down, Kirsten considered. She had no desire to back down. It needed saying.

'He wasn't always eighty-four, but obviously he was always an extremist. I'd have thought you, of all people, would have the guts to stand up to him!'

The skin about the firm mouth was paled by tension. He spoke through his teeth, his accent more pronounced. 'I already explained why I have to comply with his wishes in this instance.'

'Because of his heart?' She shook her head. 'He would hardly have reached the age he has if it weren't good and strong.'

Terje was still sitting in the same position on the grassy bank; an arm wrapped about his bent knees, but there was nothing relaxed about him. Kirsten found a moment to wonder why she was doing this–why she couldn't seem to stop doing this–when only bare hours ago she had been prepared to go along with everything.

'You have to admit it,' she said huskily. 'You have no more desire to marry me than I have to marry you. We're just two people who happened to go to bed together at the wrong time.'

The sun was touching the rim of the horizon, sending a path of molten copper shimmering over the darkened sea. As the golden disc slowly sank from sight, bonfires began to flame into life along the shorelines. Leif put a match to their own pyre, standing back as the flames licked hungrily upwards. A burst of brilliance in the sky to the south signalled the start of the waterfront fireworks back in Bergen.

'If you feel that way, then you must do as you see fit,' said Terje unemotionally after what seemed an age.

Was this what she had really wanted? Kirsten asked herself, unable to filter her voice through the hard lump in her throat. She didn't even know any more.

He got up abruptly and moved away from her, going over to sit with his aunt, who greeted him warmly. Inger's expression was confused. Kirsten didn't wonder. It must have been obvious to anyone watching that she and Terje were involved in something far outside any normal conversational exchange.

Drawn by some instinct, she looked round to find Rune's eyes fixed on her too. She held his gaze defiantly, and saw his expression alter as if in recognition of the message she was determined to convey. He might be able to hold Terje to ransom, but he wasn't doing it with her. Not any more. She had come to her senses at last.

He was the first to look away. He suddenly seemed to have shrunk in on himself. It was probably the first time in years that his will had been opposed, Kirsten reflected hardily. A shock, perhaps, but he would get over it. Tomorrow, she would move out to a hotel until her ferry sailing on Friday.

And how was she going to tell her parents that the reconciliation was off again? came the heart-sinking thought. And it would be, of course. She had made a complete mess of everything!

She was, it seemed, the only one to be looking in Rune's direction at the moment—the only one to notice the way his head had suddenly slumped forward on his chest. She was on her feet before she even thought about it, and making for his chair, fingers reaching instinctively for the carotid pulse in his neck as her eyes registered his pallor.

There was a heartbeat still, though weak. Holding his hand up, she bent and put her cheek close to his lips, drawing a breath of pure relief when she felt the slight flutter against her skin.

'What is it?' Terje was at her back, his father and aunt close behind. 'What happened?'

'I think he just passed out,' Kirsten answered, hoping it was no worse. 'He should be laid down with his legs raised. We'll need a blanket and a cushion.'

Terje wasted no time on more questions, but went immediately to fetch the items, returning to help his father lift the still form out of the chair while Kirsten and his aunt spread the blanket on the ground. Rune looked so small and fragile laid out like that, she thought numbly, as she tucked the cushion under his feet and ankles. This was her fault for causing him further emotional upset.

His colour was beginning to return, anyway, she noted thankfully. His eyelids fluttered open, eyes dazed and blank for a moment before they focused on her face. From somewhere she dredged a smile, trying this time to convey capitulation. Right or wrong, she was taking no further risks.

Leif knelt by his father's side as he attempted to raise himself, speaking to him in tones of concern and trying to make him lie still. Terje took Kirsten by the arm and drew her aside.

'How did you come to notice his condition?' he asked.

'I just happened to be looking his way.' She hesitated, seeing no encouragement in the blue eyes, but forced herself to make the effort. 'Terje, what I said just now. I'm. . .sorry.'

He studied her for a long moment before replying, giving no indication of his thoughts. 'Does this mean you've changed your mind again?' he asked at length.

'It means,' she said, 'that I'm ready to do as your grandfather wants.'

'Merely because he suffered a fainting spell? You gave the impression just now that you cared little for his welfare.'

'I was making a point, that's all,' she claimed. 'I don't wish any harm to come to him.'

He regarded her steadily for a moment or two more before inclining his head. 'Then perhaps we should set his mind entirely at rest by making the matter official.'

Kirsten drew in a shallow breath. 'Here and now?'

'Here and now.' He gave her a dry smile. 'Fairer to Inger too—as you pointed out.'

Rune was seated once more in his chair, with Hanna fussing over him like a mother hen. Of the Torvunds themselves, only Inger showed any concern. Nils was chatting with his companion as though nothing had happened.

Terje went to speak with his grandfather, doing it quietly so that Hanna couldn't overhear. Kirsten saw Rune's head nod in agreement, and was aware of having set seal to the pact. No backing out after this; she was fully committed.

Leif made the announcement. It had been intended for later, he said, but in view of Rune's need to rest he was bringing the event forward. Stunned was the only way to describe the general reaction, Kirsten thought in the moment or two following. From the look on Georg's face, Inger wasn't the only one who had counted on marriage as an outcome of her relationship with Terje. Inger herself just sat there immobile.

Nils was the first to recover, a faint sneer on his lips as he looked from Kirsten to the man at her side. 'Congratulations,' he said. 'It must have been love at first sight!'

If Terje registered the irony, he gave no sign of it. 'Almost,' he agreed. He slid an arm about Kirsten's shoulders to draw her closer, smiling down with deliberation into her eyes. 'For both of us.'

'I hope you will both be very happy,' said Inger with a quiet dignity that made Kirsten feel even worse. 'Are you to be married here in Norway?'

'In England,' Kirsten responded. 'I still have to tell my parents.'

'But you will be living in Bergen?'

It was Terje who answered, tone dispassionate. 'Of course. Where else would we live?'

Anywhere, Kirsten imagined the other girl was thinking, that I don't have to see you. It was how she would feel herself, were she in Inger's place. Whether she could have summoned quite the same degree of outward control over her emotions was a debatable point.

Appearing somewhat bewildered, Karin offered congratulations too. From the way she was with Nils, Kirsten suspected that she would like to be in the same position, but doubted if there was any real chance of it. Nils wasn't ready for marriage with anyone.

It was a measure of Rune's debility that he actually consented to go and lie down in a bed while there was still something going on. Kirsten thought longingly of the other empty bed. The rest of them might be prepared to follow tradition and stay up for the sunrise, but she didn't have the heart for it. All she wanted right now was to be on her own.

'Would it be all right if I used the other room for an hour or two?' she asked Terje. 'I'm not up to this kind of thing.'

'Of course,' he agreed, almost too readily. 'I'll waken you in time to see the sunrise.'

She would have preferred that he offer to accompany her, but there was little chance of that. He had to make his peace with Inger, for one thing. What exactly he would tell her she didn't know, and at the moment didn't particularly care.

The bedroom was warm. Kirsten opened a window before lying down fully clothed on the blanket covering the mattress. There was another blanket if she needed it, and a pillow, but no sheets. Obviously the beds were made up only as and when needed, and the need hadn't been anticipated tonight.

Supplied with blankets of their own, the others would doze where they were, she supposed. The night was fine, the fire still burning, the sunrise several hours away still. St John's Day was a national holiday, so they could all catch up on their sleep when they got home. Perhaps next year she might manage to stick it out herself. Next year...

She dreamed about Terje and the night they had spent together in Trondheim, only this time it was different because it was their honeymoon and he was telling her he loved her. She slid her arms about his neck to draw him closer as he kissed her, coming awake with a jerk to the realisation that the lips on hers were no figment of a dream but real live flesh—that the man kissing her was not Terje but Nils.

'What are you doing?' she gasped, tearing her mouth away from his. 'Stop it, Nils!'

'I don't want to stop,' he said tersely. 'You owe me some repayment for the way you used me!'

'I didn't use you,' she protested, trying to push him away and not succeeding. 'I came out with you because you asked me.'

'Knowing that Terje would go to any lengths to stop me from taking you away from him too!' His eyes glittered in the semi-darkness. 'He only wants you because you look like Jean. I hope you realise that.'

'And you only wanted her because he did,' she retorted thickly. 'You hate him, don't you, Nils? You're eaten up with jealousy because you see him as so much further up the ladder than you are yourself.'

The glitter increased. 'I have no reason to be jealous of any Burland!' he declared. 'Jean came to me because I could satisfy her better than Terje ever could. Just as I can satisfy you too.'

A hand clamped on each upper arm, he brought his head down again to find her mouth with his. The kiss was far from rough; he was using every ounce of technique he had to make her respond to him, Kirsten realised. Only it wasn't working because she felt nothing for him. She refused to put up a struggle. The more passive she was, the sooner he would stop trying.

Whether Nils had neglected to close the bedroom door, or it was opened very quietly, she never knew. The first intimation of another presence in the room was when Nils was suddenly jerked away from her. Terje looked ready to kill, she thought, coming sharply upright as the two men faced each other. His face was pale beneath the tan, his jaw rigid, eyes like cold steel.

He spoke in Norwegian, but the tone of voice needed no translation. Nils responded in like vein, a sneer on his lips as he gesticulated in Kirsten's direction. She saw Terje's fist clench, his whole arm tense for the instinctive punch, then he took a hold on himself, indicating the door with a clipped command. '*Ute!*'

There was a brief moment when it seemed that Nils might defy the injunction, then he smiled and shrugged as if to say it wasn't worth the effort, and strolled from the room. Green eyes met blue, flinching at the sheer impact of the icy gaze.

'I don't know what Nils just told you,' she said, 'but it isn't the way it looked.'

'How many interpretations can there be?' Terje demanded. 'You were making no attempt to stop him from kissing you.'

'I didn't want to incite him to even more of an effort,' she claimed, thinking even as she said it how utterly weak and implausible it sounded. 'I hoped he would lose interest if I refused to show any of my own.' She made an appealing little gesture. 'You can't really believe I was enjoying it!'

'I believe what I see,' he said grimly. 'And what I already know to be true. It was obvious that you were drawn to Nils from the beginning.'

'No, I wasn't.' Kirsten tried not to over-emphasise the denial. 'Not in any way.' She searched the unrelenting features with a sense of despair. 'If Nils were the one I wanted, we wouldn't be in the position we're in now.'

'A woman can want more than one man,' came the hard response. 'Just as a man might have a need of more than one woman. What I won't do is share.'

'There's no question of sharing.' She sought desperately for some way to convince him. 'Terje, I only *look* like Jean. I know how you felt about her, but—'

'You have no idea how I felt about her,' he clipped. 'Jean is in the past, our concern is with the present.' He paused, drawing in a harsh breath. 'You stay away from Nils! Is that clear?'

She gazed at him helplessly, hardly knowing what to say. He wasn't going to believe her, no matter *what* she said.

'If there's no trust between us, then there's no point in continuing,' she got out.

'We have to continue,' he said. 'Or are you saying that Rune's well-being means nothing to you after all?'

'Of course it does. Why else would I have agreed to this charade if it didn't?' Her voice was impassioned. 'I still have no real proof that opposition might stress him enough to cause a heart attack, but I accept the possibility.'

'Perhaps you would like to see his medical records by way of confirmation?' Terje suggested shortly. 'Last night he only lost temporary consciousness. Six months ago he was in Intensive Care for a week, and hospitalised for three weeks more. Stress is the last thing he must have.'

It was a moment or two before Kirsten could find her voice. 'Why didn't you tell me that in the first place?'

He shrugged, face shuttered. 'Because I didn't want to bring *too* much pressure to bear on you. But you see now why I had to do as he asked?'

'Of course. You couldn't do anything else.' And neither, Kirsten reflected fatalistically, could she. They had both brought the situation about, and must both make the best they could of it.

So why not start with a little honesty? came the thought. Why not let him know how she really felt? Was her pride so vital to her that she couldn't make that small sacrifice?

'You think I only agreed to marry you because of your grandfather,' she said before she could change her mind, 'but it isn't the whole truth, Terje.' She took a moment to gather her courage, forcing herself to look him in the eye regardless of the frigidity still there. 'The thing is–I love you.'

For a second or two there was no reaction at all; he just continued to regard her with the same chilly appraisal. His laugh when it came was short.

'Of course you do. In exactly the same way I love you. We have that much to be grateful for.'

'I mean it,' Kirsten insisted. 'I really do love you, Terje!'

The scepticism remained. 'Making love with another man is a very strange way of showing it.'

Anger cut through the hurt; he just didn't want to know! 'I thought it was Nils who was jealous of you!' she flung at him bitterly. 'But I'm beginning to wonder if it's the other way round. You're obsessed by him!'

The ice gave way to a sudden flaring anger of his own. He took a step towards her, then pulled himself up, teeth coming together with an audible snap. 'Then you had better make certain that I have no further cause,' he said with control.

Further protestation was obviously a waste of time, Kirsten acknowledged hopelessly. She couldn't really blame him too much for mistrusting her. The evidence was too damning.

'Why did you come anyway?' she asked, abandoning the issue.

'Why would you think?' he returned sardonically. 'Go back to sleep. It isn't sunrise yet.'

He was gone before she could draw breath to answer, closing the door quietly behind him. Not that he would have stayed, even if she had begged him to, she suspected. Nils had a lot to answer for, and she was going to make sure he did answer. There was no excuse for his behaviour

She must have slept again eventually. This time when she opened her eyes it was to find Leif about to waken her.

'The sun will be over the mountains in about ten minutes,' he said. 'I thought you would want to see it.' His smile was tentative. 'It was perhaps a little soon to introduce you to our ways.'

There was no way she could explain that her tiredness had been more emotional than physical, Kirsten thought as he went from the room. Although it would have been better if she had stayed up. The fact that it was Leif and not Terje who had come to waken her underlined the latter's continuing estrangement. It was going to be an uphill struggle to find any kind of level footing again.

Feeling badly in need of a shower and change of clothing, but with time and opportunity only for a splash of cold water on her face and fingers through her hair, she went out to where the rest of the party were finishing off last night's left-overs.

With the possible exception of Hanna, everyone looked remarkably fresh, Kirsten thought. Terje was talking with Georg, and didn't appear to have noticed her arrival. Either that, or he was ignoring her.

Nils gave her a deliberate smile that was seen and obviously misinterpreted by Karin, whose face turned stony. She would be better off without a man of Nils's nature, Kirsten reflected, but it was doubtful if she saw him as he really was.

Rune was the only one missing as the sun came creeping into view to bring both land and sea back to life. He was watching it through the bedroom window, said Leif when she asked if he was all right.

'He slept quite well,' he confirmed. 'There appear to be no after-effects. It isn't the first time he fainted away like that.'

'Terje told me about his condition,' Kirsten said softly.

'So you understand why it is so imperative that he is not distressed.' Leif sounded wry. 'I suppose it might be said that he already lived longer than most, but I would like to see him achieve his desire.'

'His century? Yes, Terje told me that too. I hope he makes it.'

'His doctors believe he has a chance through strength of will power alone,' came the faintly humorous reply. He paused, glancing Kirsten's way with a certain diffidence. 'It would be good for him to be assured of a future generation.'

It was an effort to keep both tone and face from reflecting her emotional conflict. 'I dare say he will be.' She added swiftly, 'I understand you're getting married again yourself.'

He accepted the change of subject without demur. 'You consider me too old to start again?'

Kirsten laughed, glad of the excuse. 'Hardly. You're still in the prime of life!'

'*Mange takk.*' He was smiling too. 'Margot tells me the same.'

'I look forward to meeting her.'

'Unfortunately, she's in Oslo for the next week,' he said. 'But I'll bring her to England with me when I accompany Terje.' He was silent for a moment or two, his expression contemplative. 'How much of the truth will you be telling your parents?' he asked at length.

'As little as possible,' she admitted. 'My mother would be destroyed if she knew I'd gone to bed with Terje at all, much less in your home.' It was her turn to slant a wry glance. 'I still feel bad about that.'

'I already told you there is no need. Rune was my only concern.'

The words came to her lips before she could stop them. 'Would he have approved if Terje had married Inger?'

Leif lifted his shoulders. 'The question never arose.'

'But she would be very suitable,' Kirsten insisted masochistically.

'Well, yes.' He sounded uncomfortable. 'But I don't think Terje had considered marriage at all before. . .'

'Before I came along and put him in a position where he had to,' she finished as he hesitated. 'I should never have come, Leif. None of this would have happened if I'd minded my own business.'

'It *was* your business,' he said. 'And I'm very glad that you came.'

But was Terje? she asked herself hollowly.

With the sun up, and the food finished, it was time to go. The Torvunds left first, with Nils and his girlfriend in the lead. From the way they were both reacting, there had been some kind of disagreement during the last half-hour, Kirsten judged. Perhaps Karin wasn't besotted enough, after all, to be unaware of Nils's shortcomings.

'Are you ready?' asked Terje at her back, and she turned to meet the cynical regard.

'To go, yes,' she said. 'But not to continue this way. For the last time, I wasn't offering Nils any encouragement. I don't care what it looked like! There's such a thing as circumstantial evidence.'

'There's such a thing as concealing the fact that the two of you met for lunch yesterday,' he rejoined. 'Or would you deny that too?'

Nils really was doing his utmost to tear them apart, Kirsten thought ruefully. 'It wasn't arranged,' she began, and saw his lip curl.

'Spare me the excuses. Just remember what I told you. If you ever have anything to do with him again, I'll—'

'What?' she prompted, giving way to rancour as he broke off abruptly. 'Are Norwegians into wife-beating?'

The expression on his face was enough to shut her up. She made an impulsive gesture of apology. 'That was crass.'

'But not beyond the realms of possibility,' came the curt response. 'You could drive a man to violence all too easily.'

She didn't believe him; he wasn't the kind to lose control. His behaviour under pressure a few hours ago proved that.

'I think we have to make a new start,' she said, trying to be rational. 'We can't go on this way.'

The blond head inclined in terse agreement. 'No, we can't. So, what would you like to do today?'

'I thought you'd want to go straight to bed,' She bit her lip at the look in his eyes. 'To catch up on your sleep, I meant.'

'I'm sure of it.' He shook his head. 'I'm not tired.'

'Then you decide.' She'd had enough of making overtures. 'It's *your* national holiday.'

He made no reply to that; there was, she supposed, no reply worth making. She felt utterly alienated.

Rune came out from the cottage to climb into the car unaided. He looked so old in the bright morning sunlight, every wrinkle emphasised. Meeting his eyes for a fleeting moment, Kirsten was taken aback to see him incline his head in brief recognition. An improvement, if still very far from a welcome. She doubted if he would ever really accept the liaison, even though he was the one insisting on it.

Terje waited until the other car was on its way before getting behind the wheel of his own vehicle. The next time she visited the cottage, she would be a Bruland herself, Kirsten realised. She could only hope for a better relationship than they had right now.

They drove the first mile or so in silence. Gazing out of her window at the newly awakened and superbly lovely landscape, Kirsten remembered the times she had imagined being here like this in her grandmother's homeland. Apart from the scenery, nothing had turned out the way she had anticipated. But then, reality rarely did live up to expectations.

The sudden drawing up of the car at the roadside jerked her out of her introspection. Terje sat for a moment gazing out through the windscreen, hands at rest on the wheel.

'This is no good,' he declared. He turned to look at her, searching her face. 'I want to believe what you tell me.'

'You can,' she urged. 'You really can, Terje. Nils means nothing to me. There was no arrangement to meet yesterday. I bumped into him by accident, and he insisted on taking me to lunch. That was all there was to it.'

The blue eyes held hers for a long moment more, narrowed and intent, then he nodded briefly, and put the car into gear again.

Not quite the reconciliation she might have hoped for, thought Kirsten despondently, but a step in the right direction, she supposed. Telling him again that she loved him might be another, but she didn't think he wanted to hear it.

CHAPTER TEN

CONVERSATION had picked up by the time they arrived back at the house, although a certain restraint still lingered. It was no surprise, to Kirsten at least, to find that Rune had taken to his bed again as soon as he reached home. He had looked so debilitated this morning.

'He's of an age where he should reconcile himself to spending St John's night in the comfort of home,' Leif acknowledged, 'but he refuses to submit.'

The same uncompromising attitude that Terje sometimes displayed, Kirsten reflected. And one he would have to relinquish wholesale if they were to make anything at all of this marriage of theirs.

He had gone straight upstairs himself on arrival, leaving her in some doubt as to just how they were to spend the day. She would have liked to go sailing herself, but she had told him to do the choosing.

'Is it all right if I use the sauna?' she asked Leif, adding hurriedly, 'Providing you weren't intending to use it yourself, of course.'

He shook his head, smiling a little. 'Take as long as you wish.'

Like his grandfather's opposite, Terje's door was closed. It was still closed some five minutes later when she passed it to reach the sauna-room at the far end of the corridor. It was possible, she supposed, that he had changed his mind and gone to bed after all. Yesterday at this time she might have joined him, but spontaneity of that nature was right out of the window now.

The sauna was rather larger than she had imagined, with reclining benches along two walls. She dialled a medium heat setting, and discarded her robe to stretch out on the furthest bench, listening to the soft hiss of steam filtering in through the vents.

The Scandinavians were obsessed to the point of fanaticism with deep-down cleanliness, but it wasn't a bad characteristic to have. She could feel the perspiration beginning to run already. Half an hour would probably be as much as she could stand. After that would come a cold shower to close her pores again, and that wonderful feel of physical well-being that always followed. She needed that stimulation more than she had ever done.

Half dozing, mind wandering at will, she stiffened in shock as the door opened. Terje came in swiftly and closed it again before too much steam could escape. The while towel knotted about his hips emphasised the golden tan of his skin, the lean muscularity of torso and limb.

'I want you,' he said simply.

Kirsten found her voice stuck in her throat. Her stomach muscles contracted as he dropped the towel. He was aroused already, and becoming more so by the second as he surveyed her own nude length.

He came and knelt at her side, eyes on her face as he slowly, and with infinite lightness of touch, traced the curve from temple down to the point of her jaw, then on down the taut stretch of her throat to linger for a moment or two at the vulnerable hollow, with the pulse beating wildly beneath his fingers.

She kept her eyes open, her body motionless, watching his expression as he ran those same long fingers along the fine boning of her shoulder and upper arm, catching her breath when he drifted them across to explore each breast in turn, and in intimate detail. Her nipples were aching, throbbing peaks, begging the touch of his lips, the fire of his tongue, the bite of his teeth. She moaned deep in her throat, back arching involuntarily to the tantalising, seductive caresses.

His hand moved on to follow the curve of her waist and over the fluttering skin of her abdomen, utterly sensitive in its passage. She quivered as he stroked down her groin, thighs parting of their own accord to allow him total command of her whole being, the back of her own hand pressed across her mouth to stifle the sounds he was wringing from her.

But that wasn't all. Starting again at her temple, his lips followed the same slow, stroking passage downwards, sucking gently at first and then with increasing strength on each tender, peaking nub of flesh until she felt as if her very essence was being drawn from her. Her fingers curled into her palms, nails biting into her flesh as he moved on down over stomach and abdomen to deliver the most intimate and powerful caress of all, opening her mouth in a silent scream at the sheer ecstatic agony of it. Too much, she thought wildly. Far, far too much!

Then he was over her and above her, sliding inside her to fill her with his masculine hardness, lifting himself on his elbows to watch her face as he claimed total possession. Slicked with perspiration, his whole body gleamed; his skin felt like oiled silk beneath her fingers. They were joined as one, and it was wonderful. She wanted to stay here like this forever.

His first compelling movement dispelled that notion. Her lips lifted instinctively in answer, her limbs wrapping themselves about him, her whole body answering the driving domination. She belonged to this man—every last minute part of her. She wanted no one else but him.

Climax came simultaneously for them both. Head thrown back, face contorted, Terje stayed rigid for a pulsing second or two before collapsing down on to her to bury his face in her shoulder. Kirsten lay supine under him, welcoming his weight, his vulnerability. For these few moments he was all hers.

'We must make the most of today,' he murmured after a while. 'I can take no further time before we leave on Friday.'

'I wouldn't expect it,' Kirsten denied, stifling the urge to tell him she would as soon spend the day right here. 'I can find plenty to occupy me.'

'I'm sure of it.' He levered himself abruptly up and away from her, reaching for the towel he had discarded and fastening it about his hips once more. He didn't look at her. 'You'll need time to dry your hair. I'll see you downstairs in an hour from now.'

She let him go without protest. He had had all he wanted from her for the moment. This would probably be the last time they were alone together before their departure, she thought hollowly. She couldn't go to his room, and she doubted if he would come to hers.

If her parents were to be convinced that the two of them had fallen madly in love—and that was the only thing her mother was going to even begin to understand—then they would both need to put on an act. If Terje stayed in England over the weekend, that meant keeping up appearances over two whole days. She wasn't even sure of her own capabilities, much less his.

The cold shower revived her in body if not in spirit. Warm and sunny as it had already been outside, she decided that shorts were the order of the day. If Terje had anything in mind that called for more formal wear, she could always come up and change again.

He was wearing shorts himself, she discovered when she eventually went downstairs–white like her own, with a blue T-shirt that almost matched his eyes.

'Great minds think alike,' she said lightly, determined to do as he had suggested and make the most of the day that lay ahead. 'Where are we going?'

'I arranged to meet some friends on the waterfront,' he returned. 'The news will travel fast, and I'd prefer them to hear it first hand.'

'How do you want to play it?' Kirsten asked, and saw his lips slant.

'Just be natural,' he returned with irony. 'They won't be expecting any demonstrations.'

'My mother will,' she said, seizing the opportunity. 'Subtle ones, at any rate.'

'So we'll have to provide her with some. It shouldn't prove too difficult. A little holding of hands, the tender glance, the snatched kiss when supposedly no one is looking–isn't that the way true love declares itself?'

'I wouldn't know,' she said huskily. She turned abruptly away. 'I'm ready to go, if you are.'

Bergen was scarcely less busy than it had been the day before, with as many locals as tourists around. Terje parked the car in a side-street, and cut through two more to reach the waterfront.

The small section of land between the two jutting piers held an open-air café that was already crowded with early diners. At first glance every table appeared occupied to its full capacity, but someone called Terje's name, and an arm was waved from somewhere in the middle of the throng.

Kirsten pinned a smile to her lips as they threaded their way through to the table. There were four people seated there, but only one of them female–a woman some five or six years older than her herself, who looked at her with typical feminine speculation. Hers was the only name that stuck in Kirsten's mind during the following introductions, although it did penetrate that she was married to one of the men.

'Kirsten is my cousin from England,' Terje finished, adding smoothly, 'And soon to be my wife.'

Reactions were predictable, especially when it was realised that she hadn't even been in Bergen a full week as yet. Kirsten could hardly believe it herself. A lifetime seemed to have passed since she had stepped off the ferry on to Norwegian soil.

All of them around the same age as Terje, and equally fit, the men were hiking and climbing companions, she gathered. There was an easy rapport between them all.

'Do you climb too?' she asked Benta as the men lapsed into Norwegian. 'Or is that purely a male hobby?'

'I used to climb,' the other ackowledged. 'But we have two children now, and my weekends are no longer as free. You are an enthusiast yourself?'

Kirsten shook her head. 'I could never see a great deal of point in hauling myself up a mountain only to come down again.'

'It's the challenge,' Benta defended. 'The sense of satisfaction on reaching the top of a difficult ascent. There are few moments better!'

Kirsten could think of at least one. So, she was sure, on catching the twinkle in the other woman's eyes, could Benta herself.

'Shall you not miss England when you come here to live?' the Norwegian woman asked. 'You must find our ways very different.'

'It will be strange at first, I expect,' Kirsten acknowledged, trying to sound buoyant about it, 'but there are compensations.'

'With Terje the most important of all, of course.'

The comment was more than a little tongue-in-cheek, and was answered in the same vein. 'But of course!'

Benta dropped her voice to say more seriously, 'You will be much envied when the news becomes known. There are many who would like to marry Terje.'

Kirsten could well believe it. Looks apart, he was quite a catch. She wondered how many of those would-be wives he had made love to in his time; he certainly hadn't gained such expertise without plenty of practice.

Food was ordered and eaten. Afterwards, Benta's husband, Rolf, suggested that they all spend the rest of the afternoon on his boat. The other two men declined the invitation, but Terje agreed at once, without consulting Kirsten. Not that she had any objection, she admitted, but he could at least have gone through the motions. Benta's only stipulation was that they must be back by four-thirty, as they were to eat *middag* at her mother's home.

The boat turned out to be a sizeable cabin cruiser berthed along the shorter of the two piers. Seated in the cushioned and comfortable well as they moved down the Vågen towards more open water, Kirsten made herself relax. Apart from climbing, she intended taking an active part in all Terje's weekend pursuits. Come the winter, she might even manage to surprise him with her skiing ability too. Whatever it took, this marriage was going to work. It *had* to work.

Almost as if catching her thought, Terje glanced round from where he stood at Rolf's side in the cockpit, his eyes riveted to her face for a brief moment before he turned away again. Standing there with his back to her, balancing easily with the movement of the boat, he looked so self-sufficient, so contained. He didn't need her, that was certain. He didn't need any woman, except for the one purpose. He was marrying her only because his grandfather commanded it.

Reaching the wider waters of the Byfjorden, they turned along the mainland coastline with its colourful little settlements and low, pine-clad hills. The quality of light was superb, the distances needle-sharp. A photographer's paradise, Kirsten thought, regretting her lack of a camera.

'We none of us knew that Terje had English relatives,' Benta remarked after a while, giving way to the curiosity she had managed so far to suppress. 'How did it happen?'

'His grandfather's sister married my grandfather, and the families lost touch over the years,' Kirsten acknowledged. 'I simply decided it was time we got together.'

Benta laughed. 'You certainly did that! And now you and Terje are to close up the circle again. Did you know as soon as you met that it would be this way?'

'Not instantly.' Kirsten kept her tone light. 'It took a couple of days to sink in.'

'You will be marrying in England, of course?'

'Oh, yes. And soon.' Kirsten couldn't bring herself to say just *how* soon. 'Terje doesn't want to wait very long,' she added by way of preparation.

Benta laughed again. 'When lightning strikes there is no resisting it! Rolf and I were also quick to know our minds—although perhaps not quite as quick.'

But they hadn't had Rune behind them, thought Kirsten wryly.

A small, motorised skiff had come up on their starboard side and was keeping pace. The boy at the tiller could be no more than twelve or thirteen, Kirsten judged, while the other boy and girl were even younger. They were all laughing and waving. She waved back, admiring the helmsman's skilful handling of the little craft. Young he might be, but he was obviously born to the water. All the same, they seemed a little too far out from the land for such a small boat.

Sweeping the skiff around, the boy headed it into the spreading wake from their own larger craft, yelling with delight as they rode the swell. A moment later he came racing back to do the same thing again, this time making the turn even faster.

'The girl has no life-jacket,' said Benta, also watching the performance. 'She has no business being on the water without a jacket!'

'Do you think we should try and stop them doing that?' asked Kirsten worriedly as the skiff came up once more. 'He could turn it over.'

It happened almost before the words had left her mouth, although not quite in the way she had predicted. From the way the prow of the boat suddenly reared into the air, it had to have hit some hidden object in the water. Too shocked to scream, all three children were spilled overboard by the sheer force of the impact. Kirsten watched in horror as the boat turned over in the air and came crashing down on top of them.

Rolf brought the cruiser around in a wide sweep, cutting the engine as they neared the upturned skiff. The two boys looked to have escaped any injury, but there was no sign of the girl.

Kicking off his sandals, Terje dived straight in, surfacing moments later with the child in his arms. She was obviously unconscious, her face pale beneath its tan. Safe within their life-jackets, the two boys looked much the same colour.

Both Kirsten and Benta leaned over the side to take the small limp body, leaving Terje free to go back for the boys, who both seemed too dazed to do anything for themselves.

The girl wasn't breathing, and Kirsten could feel no pulse. Without pausing to think about it, she placed the water-sleeked head in position and gave the prescribed two inflations before beginning chest compression.

Kneeling at the girl's head, Benta indicated that she would continue the mouth-to-mouth, cutting the compressions between breaths from fifteen to five, and vastly increasing the supply of oxygen to the brain. Working as a team, they counted off the seconds, pausing for a pulse check at one minute.

'We have a heartbeat!' Kirsten exclaimed in relief, feeling the throb beneath her fingers. She sat back on her heels as Benta continued to give mouth-to-mouth, ready to spell her if it became necessary.

The livid bruise on the girl's forehead told its own story. There was no depression of the bone, but there could still be a fracture, although it was more likely to be the shock of sudden immersion in ice-cold water that had caused her heart to stop.

A choking cough heralded success on Benta's part too. She turned the child swiftly into the recovery position to allow any inhaled water to drain from her mouth, looking at Kirsten with a smile as she wiped the back of her hand across her damp forehead.

'We make a good team together,' she said. 'Now we must get her to hospital.'

They were already under way, Rolf at the wheel. Terje had taken the two boys down to the cabin, Kirsten assumed.

'I think we'd best leave her where she is for the moment, don't you?' she said. 'Perhaps a blanket to cover her?'

'I will fetch one,' agreed the other.

She disappeared below. A moment or two later, Terje came up carrying the blanket.

'Benta is staying with the boys,' he said. 'They're both

of them feeling nauseous.' He knelt down beside Kirsten to cover the girl's slight form, watching the gentle but regular rise and fall of her breathing for a moment before sitting back on his heels the way Kirsten was doing herself. The blue eyes were appraising.

'Where did you learn to resuscitate?'

'First-aid course with the St John Ambulance Brigade,' she said. 'My uncle's suggestion. Dental patients have been known to collapse through sheer terror.'

His smile warmed her. 'Even when they only need a scale and polish?'

'It's the chair that does it,' she claimed, smiling back. 'Plus an over-active imagination in some cases. There was a film a few years ago where an ex-Nazi tried to extract information from a man by drilling his teeth right down to the nerve without anaesthetic. We had several cancelled appointments the day after it was shown on television for the first time.'

Terje laughed, revealing a set of teeth without defect. 'Your uncle should have sued the film company.'

'Knowing him, he probably considered it.' Kirsten turned her glance back to the girl, willing her to regain consciousness. 'How long before we reach harbour?'

'Another ten minutes. But an ambulance will be waiting. Rolf called through on the radio.'

The girl stirred suddenly, whimpering under her breath. Kirsten bent and stroked the smooth young cheek. 'It's all right,' she comforted her. 'You're safe now.' She added to Terje, 'Perhaps you'd better tell her in Norwegian too.'

He did so, voice gentle. The girl's eyes flickered, and finally came all the way open, but they had a blank look about them that made Kirsten's heart sink afresh. She continued to stroke her cheek, hoping against hope that they had been in time. Brain damage occurred after ninety seconds without oxygen. It had taken longer than that to get her on board, but the coldness of the water might have retarded the process.

'You *are* different from Jean,' Terje said softly, watching her. 'She had little true tenderness.'

Kirsten kept her eyes down, her voice low. 'But you still loved her?'

'I believed I did at the time. The truth of it is that my pride suffered the worst blow.'

Benta appeared in the cabin doorway. 'How is she?' she asked.

'Conscious,' Kirsten confirmed, 'but not responding. She could be in shock still.'

Terje got to his feet, leaving a small puddle of water from his sodden clothing. 'I'll go and take care of the boys,' he said. 'You two can keep watch here.'

Kirsten had the feeling that he already regretted opening up the way he had just now, and was seizing the opportunity to escape any further temptation to confide in her. It made little difference in the long run whether he had loved Jean or not, she supposed, but it somehow helped to know that he hadn't

They made the harbour to find a whole crowd waiting with the ambulance. All three children were taken on board, the girl on a stretcher. Terje had obtained an address from the boys, and would inform the parents, he told the ambulance crew.

'My mother's house is out towards that area,' said Benta when she heard where the children came from. 'Rolf and I will go and tell the parents.'

Terje relinquished the task without argument. Kirsten didn't blame him. Breaking such news was no easy undertaking.

Driving home in the wet shorts and shirt didn't appear

to bother him, uncomfortable though they must be. They were almost at the house before it occurred to her to ask what had happened to the childrens' boat.

'It sank,' he said. 'The whole front end was gone. They must have hit a log. It was only by luck that they weren't all killed.'

If the girl did turn out to be brain damaged, it might have been a kinder end in her case, Kirsten reflected. She could imagine how the mother was going to feel when Benta and Rolf turned up with the news.

'I like your friends,' she commented. 'Especially Benta. Have you know them long?'

'Rolf and I were in school together. Benta I met when he did. They were married more than eight years ago.' A smile touched his lips. 'She believes all men should be married by the time they reach thirty. She had begun to despair of me.'

She would despair even more if she knew the truth, thought Kirsten ruefully.

Neither Leif nor Rune was in evidence when they arrived, but Leif put in an appearance for *middag*. His father had been up in the afternoon, he said, but had decided to eat in his room.

'I'm worried about him,' he admitted. 'He seems so listless.'

'It's my fault,' claimed Kirsten unhappily. 'The whole thing is my fault! I shouldn't be here.'

'His heart attack a few months ago was hardly your fault,' Lief consoled her. 'Last night was too much for him. If there is any fault to be found, it must lie with me for not insisting that he stay home.' He lightened his tone. 'What did the two of you do with your day?'

Terje seemed disinclined to go into any detail, so it was

left to Kirsten to explain about the accident, expressing her fears for the girl.

'If I telephoned the hospital, do you think they would tell me how she is?' she asked. 'In England, they only give out information to relatives.'

'Here too, I think,' said Leif, 'but we can try. Perhaps if you explain your involvement in the child's rescue, the rules may be stretched.

'I know the paediatrician,' Terje cut in. 'I'll ask her.'

Kirsten wondered fleetingly how old the paediatrician was, then sighed inwardly and dismissed the question. That way lay paranoia

Terje telephoned the hospital as soon as the meal was over, returning to report that the girl was going to make a full recovery.

'You and Benta saved both her life and her mind between you,' he said. 'The mother wishes to meet with you and thank you personally.'

'It really isn't necessary,' Kirsten protested. 'We only did what anyone would have done.'

'But not everyone would have known *what* to do,' Leif pointed out. 'You would surely not refuse the mother an opportunity to express her gratitude?'

'I'll take you to see her before we leave,' Terje declared, making the decision for her. 'Benta must come too.'

Benta would probably feel the same way she did about it, thought Kirsten resignedly. She would be happy just to know that the child had suffered no permanent damage.

Left alone with her father-in-law-to-be when Terje went up to see his grandfather, she found conversation no problem. Leif was an easy and interesting person to be with–knowledgeable on so many subjects, yet a good listener too.

'If you like Grieg's music, there are recitals every day at the Rasmus Meyer art galleries during the summer,' he told her, 'and one tomorrow evening at Troldhaugen itself. Terje should take you. It may still be possible to obtain tickets.'

'I already have them,' said his son, returning to the room.

Kirsten looked at him assessingly as he took a seat, struck by something odd in his voice. He returned her gaze without expression.

'How did you find Rune?' asked Leif.

'Resigned,' came the answer. 'He's come to the conclusion that it's time for the past to be buried.' He paused, then went on levelly, 'He doesn't pretend to condone our behaviour, but he withdraws his demand that we marry.'

Kirsten struggled to keep both face and voice from reflecting her emotions. 'What made him change his mind again so suddenly?'

The shrug was brief. 'All I know is that he has changed it.'

Leif said quietly, 'So what happens now?'

It was Kirsten who answered. 'We breathe a sigh of relief. It would never have worked out anyway.'

'And what do I tell my sister and family when it was only last night that they heard you were to be married?'

'I don't know,' she said, not really caring. 'The truth, perhaps.'

'You'll still be taking the ferry on Friday?' asked Terje dispassionately.

'I suppose so.' She hadn't got round to thinking that far ahead. 'If I arrived home early, my parents would want to know why.'

'And you would be reluctant to have *them* know the truth,' said Leif drily.

'Yes, I would. There's no reason why they should have to know anything at all.'

'If they decide to take up my invitation to visit, they may hear about it regardless,' he pointed out.

'It's doubtful if they ever will come here,' she said. 'It always was. All Dad ever really wanted was to straighten things out. Be honest about it,' she went on before he could comment, 'you're not exactly eager to make the trip yourself. And why should you be? You and my father would have little in common.'

Leif made no attempt to contradict her. 'What about you? Shall we be seeing you again?'

Her laugh was brittle. 'I think I caused enough problems already.'

Terje got abruptly to his feet. 'I'm going for a walk,' he announced.

Kirsten steeled herself against the urge to go after him as he went from the room. He had wanted her this morning, and might want her still, but he was thankful to be free of the commitment, that was obvious. She should be thankful too.

'Is this really the way you want it to be?' asked Leif softly. 'I believed my son meant more to you than just a passing fancy.'

'It seems not,' she said. 'If Terje marries anyone, it should be Inger.'

'If he wanted to marry Inger, he would have done it before now.' Leif paused, watching her face, then gave a resigned shrug. 'I can only apologise for the distress my father has caused you. You will excuse me if I go to him?'

'Of course.'

Left alone, Kirsten sat in bleak contemplation of a future without Terje. She had known him less than a week, yet he had become the most important person in her life. The thought of never seeing him again was insupportable.

She stiffened when he said her name from the doorway,

but it was too late for concealment with the tears already
overflowing. She scrubbed the back of a hand across them
as he moved towards her, turning a defiant face up to him.

'What?'

There was sudden realisation in the blue eyes as he studied her. He drew her upright, holding her close to kiss each
damp cheek before finding her mouth with a passion that
said far more than words. Kirsten clung to him, not even
trying to think—kissing him back with a feverish intensity.

'I won't let you go,' he said against her lips. '*Jeg elsker
deg.*'

'I love you too,' she responded shakily, understanding
the meaning if not the words. 'But you know that already.
I told you last night.'

'I didn't know what to believe last night,' he admitted.
'Finding you with Nils was like history repeating itself.'
He shook his head as she made to speak, his smile wry. 'I
allowed jealousy to overrule my judgement, and said some
regrettable things.'

'It doesn't matter,' she said. 'Nothing matters now.' She
looked at him for a long, searching moment, still not wholly
sure of him. 'Where do we go from here?'

'To England,' he rejoined. 'As arranged.'

'But there's no necessity now that Rune backed down.'

'You think he was the only reason I asked you to marry
me? It might not have been quite as soon, but I already had
it in mind. All I needed was to know that you had the same
feelings for me.' He cupped her face in his hands, looking
deep into her eyes. 'I've waited a long time for you, *min
yndling*. You're everything I ever hoped to find.'

Her smile was tremulous. 'I'll try to live up to expectations.'

'You already went far beyond them.' His eyes kindled

as he gazed at her. 'I can't stop wanting you. You light a fire inside me every time I look at you.'

'No more than you do to me.' She drew in a long slow breath. 'How do you think Rune will take it?'

'We'll go now and see.'

Kirsten hung back. 'Supposing he has another attack with all this chopping and changing?'

Terje smiled and shook his head. 'He won't.'

'You can't be sure,' she insisted. 'He must have been under strain all day thinking things through.'

'He had no change of mind. I persuaded him to let me tell you that he had.'

She gazed at him in puzzlement. 'Why?'

'Because I wanted to know how you really felt about me.' He added wryly, 'Your reaction wasn't what I was hoping for.'

'I was devastated,' she confessed. 'I just didn't dare show it. I thought you were relieved to be free.'

'That was my impression of you too. I had to leave before I gave myself away.'

'But you came back,' she said softly. 'Thank heaven, you came back!'

The blue eyes were illuminated. 'I got no further than the porch before I admitted to myself that pride was doing the driving. I came back to make you say yes to me, whatever it took.'

'And found me blubbering all over the place.'

'The most encouraging sight I could have hoped to see.'

His kiss held such tenderness, she felt tears prickling her lids again, but of happiness this time. It still wouldn't be easy facing her parents, but at least there would be no pretence. Terje loved her the way she loved him: deeply, passionately and for always.

This time she made no demur when he turned her in the

direction of the door. If Rune could bend, then so could she. The same Viking blood ran in their veins, diluted in hers, perhaps, but still a factor in common.

He was sitting in a chair at his bedroom window looking out at the mountains he had tramped and climbed in his day. Even more now, Kirsten regretted her inability to communicate with him. She watched his face as Terje spoke to him, trying to interpret his expression. Not pleasure exactly, but not hostility either.

On impulse, she went down on a knee to take one gnarled old hand and press it lightly to her cheek, looking straight into the faded blue eyes.

'I'm where I belong,' she said. 'With a man I love. Will you give us your blessing?'

If the words meant nothing to him, the meaning must have got through. His smile was muted, but it signified acceptance.

Terje put an arm about her as she came upright again, drawing her close.

'Welcome home, Kirsten Bruland,' he said.

Welcome to Europe

NORWAY–'Europe's most beautiful secret'

Norway means 'the way to the north', the name given to 20,000 km of spectacular fjords, narrows and straits. It is a land of contrasts, boasting one of the world's most advanced technological societies along with some of Europe's most magnificent scenery in its mountains, fjords, plateaux and wilderness. In summertime, the mountains are often covered in snow, while in other parts of the country the sun never sets. The climate is surprisingly warm too, on account of the Gulf Stream–the temperature can reach 25°C in summer even in northern Norway. As you can see, the attractions of this beautiful country are manifold, and for those of you who enjoy a taste of romance and adventure it's the ideal place in which to explore.

THE ROMANTIC PAST

Norway first made its mark on the world during what has become known as the Viking Era–from around 800 to 1100

AD. The Vikings were great explorers, founded many settlements in France, Britain, Iceland and Greenland, and actually discovered America some 500 years before Columbus.

Norway was under Danish rule from 1380 to 1814, when a union with Sweden was formed. This union terminated peacefully in 1905. The Germans occupied Norway during the Second World War, although the king and government, from exile in London, continued to fight against them on the Allied side. Indeed, at this time Norway's merchant fleet was one of the largest and most modern, and the merchant navy made a valuable contribution to the Allied war effort.

A wave of nationalism after 1814, when Norway gained independence from Denmark, led to a flourishing of the arts, particularly music and literature.

Famous Norwegians include composer **Edvard Grieg**, author **Henrik Ibsen**, artist **Edvard Munch** and explorer **Roald Amundsen**.

The national costume of Norway is known as the *bunad* and, although differing slightly between areas, has common characteristics. The women's costume comprises a skirt or dress of double-shuttle woven wool and bodices or jackets of a similar or contrasting fabric worn over blouses with scarves. Traditional shoes and stockings are also worn. For the men, the *bunad* consists of a three-piece knickerbocker suit with a matching or contrasting waistcoat, a white shirt, long socks and traditional shoes. Although in the past these were everyday clothes, from around the mid-1800s they were worn, as today, mainly for festive events.

THE ROMANTIC PRESENT–pastimes for lovers...

The mention of Norway invariably conjures up images of fjords and countryside, but there is plenty to do in the country's capital, Oslo, so be sure to allow time for a visit here. Start off in the street of Karl Johans Gate, in the heart of the city, and walk to the late-19th-century **Nationalteatret** (National Theatre), a cultural centre with statues of two of Norway's most famous writers–Henrik Ibsen and Björnstjerne Björnson. Just north of here is the university of Oslo and, beyond that, the **Royal Palace**, which is not open to the public but is worth seeing nevertheless–as is the **Stortinget**, Norway's parliament. Located east of the palace, this impressive government building looks, in parts, more like a cathedral.

If you're in the mood for browsing round museums, head for the **Nasjongalleriet** (National Gallery), home to Norway's largest art collection, including 4000 paintings (the majority by Norwegian artists), as well as drawings, watercolours, engravings and prints.

Behind the **Nasjongalleriet** you'll find the **Historisk Museum**, where there is a fine collection of Viking artefacts, and if you walk diagonally from the museum's entrance you will come to the **Kunstindustrimuseum** (the Museum of Applied Art) where there is a wonderful collection of artefacts dating from the Middle Ages–a mish-mash of clothes, furniture and china.

From the centre of the city down towards the harbour is the **Akershus Fortress**, the most ancient building in the city, having been built in the early 14th century by King Haakon V. As well as being impressive to look at, the fortress contains the **Hjemmefrontmuseum**, a war museum which records Norway's role in the Resistance–quite apt,

since the building was used by the Nazis during their oc-
cupation of Oslo in the Second World War!

If you'd rather be outside, just take a stroll in the grounds
or along the ramparts, which command a lovely view of
the city.

Some of the best sightseeing, however, is actually just outside the city–for example, **Frogner Park** contains 650 statues depicting the cycle of human life by the sculptor Gustav
Vigeland, including a sixty foot monolith carved from a
single block of stone.

If you take the ferry from outside the city hall to Bygdøy,
you can see the famous polar ship *Fram*, the vessel which
carried Roald Amundsen on the first part of his journey to
the South Pole in 1911; it's beautifully preserved and visitors are allowed to climb aboard!

Near by are the **Maritime** and **Kon-Tiki** museums and the
very impressive **Vikingshiphuset** (Viking Ship Museum),
which houses three Viking burial ships dating from 800 to
900 AD, and the artefacts they contained.

As a last stop, the **Norsk Folkemuseum** (Norwegian Folk
Museum) is well worth a visit–there are over 150 reassem-
bled buildings from all over the country, dating from the
Middle Ages, and there are several interiors, including Ib-
sen's study, which looks exactly as it did when he lived in
Oslo.

And now to the hills! By taking a train up to **Frognerseter
station** and then walking for about fifteen-minutes you'll
reach the **Tryvannshøgda observation tower**, from where
there is a breathtaking view over the fjord and the city. If
you then walk down the hill you will come to the awesome
Holmenkollen ski jump, where the annual Hollmenkollen

championships take place in March. At the side of the jump there is a small museum containing a ski that's over 2,500 years old, and polar equipment used by Amundsen on his South Pole expedition.

And finally, for those of you in need of a pick-me-up after all this fresh air, why not stop off at the grand **Holmen-kollen Park Hotel**, just a short hop down from the ski jump, and take some refreshment at one of its cafés or restaurants?

Now we go from the country's capital to another lovely city–**Bergen**. No trip to Norway would be complete without a visit to its fjords, of which **Geirangerfjord**, **Sognefjord** and **Hardangerfjord** rank among the very best, and **Bergen** is a perfect base from which to explore them.

Founded in 1070, this city combines tradition with modern city life, and has many tourist attractions, including **Trold-haugen**, the home of composer **Edvard Grieg**, many museums and galleries, several attractive shops and a lively, thriving fish market. You can enjoy a wonderful view by taking a cable car up to the surrounding seven mountains, or, if you're feeling energetic, stroll along one of the many hiking trails, enjoying the wonderfully clean, fresh air.

Incidentally, in 1990 **Bergen** was voted one of the three tidiest cities in Europe–so if you're someone who likes things to be spick and span, this is the place for you!

If your holiday destination is confined to Oslo and/or the fjords, then you may not have the opportunity to visit the north of the country, but it would be a crime to pass over this beautiful part of Norway without a mention!

A five-day journey from Bergen on the **Coastal Express** steamer will take you all the way up the coast of Norway to **Kirkenes**, the country's northernmost point, beyond the Arctic Circle!

North Norway is quite unique in its consistently warm climate, due to the warm Gulf Stream, and the seasons are such that in winter it is pitch dark at midday–except for those occasions when the **Northern Lights** light up the sky!–and in summer you can ski in the hot sun in the middle of the night!

If you're visiting in summer, one of the most romantic trips in this region has to be to **Nordkapp** (the North Cape) where you and your lover can capture the magic of seeing the Midnight Sun high above the Arctic Ocean.

With all the walking and abundance of fresh air you're bound to experience wherever you are in Norway, you'll no doubt work up an appetite! The Norwegian diet is largely healthy and extremely appetising; breakfast is usually hearty, comprising cold meats, cheese, various breads, eggs, herrings, *gravlax* (marinated salmon), cereals, tea and coffee.

For lunch you might like to try *Øllebrød*–beef marinated in beer and served in pitta bread with salad–or a *pølser*, which is a long, thin hot dog served either in *brød* (bread) or rolled in a potato pancake called a *lompe*. For your evening meal you'll be spoilt for choice–in early autumn grouse, elk, pheasant and reindeer steaks served in wild mushroom sauce with peppercorns are widely available, and autumn is also the best season for seafood. For dessert, ice-cream and apple pie are very popular, and in summer the tasty sweets made from the berries that grow in the Norwegian woods are mouthwatering!

Alcohol is very expensive in Norway, and most people tend to drink beer. However, you might like to try *akevitt*, made from caraway seeds and potatoes, and very potent!

Lastly, no matter where you are in Norway, you'll be sure to want a souvenir to take home with you, and there are several to choose from. Wooden figures, bowls and dishes are very popular, as are trolls, Viking ships and costume dolls. Norway is also well-known for its pewterware–candlesticks, bowls and trays–and crystal. Of course, knitwear is a speciality–why not take home a sweater knitted in a traditional pattern to keep you cosy through the cold winter months?

DID YOU KNOW THAT...?

* Norway extends **1750 km** from south to north–the same distance from London to Athens.

* almost one quarter of Norway is covered by **forests**.

* Norway is one of the main suppliers of **crude oil** and **natural gas** to Western Europe. Other exports include **metals**, **chemicals** and **fish**.

* the Norwegian people are keen readers: every year around **40 million books** are sold–that's nearly ten per person.

* the Norwegian currency is **kroner**.

* to say 'I love you' in Norwegian, say '*Jeg elsker deg*'.

The world's bestselling romance series.

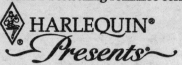

HARLEQUIN®

Presents

Seduction and Passion Guaranteed!

Introducing Jane Porter's exciting new series

**The Galván men: proud Argentine aristocrats...
who've chosen American rebels as their brides!**

IN DANTE'S DEBT
Harlequin Presents #2298

Count Dante Galván was ruthless—and though it broke Daisy's
heart she had no alternative but to hand over control of her family's
stud farm to him. She was in Dante's debt up to her ears! Daisy
knew she was far too ordinary ever to become the count's wife—
but could she resist his demands that she repay her dues in his bed?

On sale January 2003

LAZARO'S REVENGE
Harlequin Presents #2304

Lazaro Herrera has vowed revenge on Dante, his half brother, who
refuses to acknowledge his existence. When Dante's sister-in-law
Zoe arrives in Argentina, it seems the perfect opportunity. But
the clash of Zoe's blond and blue-eyed beauty with his own
smoldering dark looks creates a sexual force so strong that
Lazaro's plan begins to fall apart....

On sale February 2003

**Pick up a Harlequin Presents® novel and you will enter
a world of spine-tingling passion and
provocative, tantalizing romance!**

Available wherever Harlequin books are sold.

HARLEQUIN®

Makes any time special ®

Visit us at www.eHarlequin.com

HPGALVAN

International bestselling author

SANDRA MARTON

invites you to attend the

WEDDING *of the* YEAR

Glitz and glamour prevail in this volume
containing a trio of stories in which
three couples meet at a
high society wedding—and
soon find themselves
walking down the aisle!

Look for it in November 2002.

FALL IN LOVE
THIS WINTER
WITH
HARLEQUIN BOOKS!

In October 2002 look for these special volumes
led by *USA TODAY* bestselling authors,
and receive MOULIN ROUGE on video*!

*Retail value of $14.98 U.S. Mail-in offer. Two proofs of purchase required.
Limited time offer. Offer expires 3/31/03.

See inside these books for details.

Own MOULIN ROUGE on video!
*This exciting promotion
is available at your
favorite retail outlet.*

Only from

HARLEQUIN®
Makes any time special ®

KATE HOFFMANN

brings readers a brand-new,
spin-off to her *Mighty Quinns* miniseries

REUNITED

Keely McLain Quinn had grown up an only child—so it
was a complete shock to learn that she had six older
brothers and a father who'd never known she existed!
But Keely's turmoil is just beginning, as she discovers
the man she's fallen in love with is determined to
destroy her newfound family.

*Look for REUNITED
in October 2002.*

HARLEQUIN®
Makes any time special®

$ **Saving Money** $
Has Never Been
This Easy!

Just fill out and send in this form from any October, November and December 2002 books and we will send you a coupon booklet worth a total savings of $20.00 off future purchases of Harlequin and Silhouette books in 2003.

Yes! It's that easy!

I accept your incredible offer!
Please send me a coupon booklet:

Name (PLEASE PRINT)

Address   Apt. #

City   State/Prov.   Zip/Postal Code

In a typical month, how many
Harlequin and Silhouette novels do you read?

❏ **0-2**   ❏ **3+**

097KJKDNC7   097KJKDNDP

Please send this form to:
   In the U.S.: Harlequin Books, P.O. Box 9071, Buffalo, NY 14269-9071
   In Canada: Harlequin Books, P.O. Box 609, Fort Erie, Ontario L2A 5X3

Allow 4-6 weeks for delivery. Limit one coupon booklet per household. Must be postmarked no later than January 15, 2003.

HARLEQUIN®
Makes any time special®

Silhouette®
Where love comes alive™

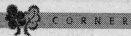